CW00719006

AUDACITY'S SONG

Jeremy Poolman was born and educated in England, but spends much of his time in the United States. His first novel, *Interesting Facts About the State of Arizona*, won Best First Published Book in the Eurasia Region of the Commonwealth Writers Prize and was acclaimed by the critics:

'A laid-back and beguiling debut novel.' *Sunday Times*

'A delight to read.' *Guardian*

'Poolman's Loopy humour is truly his own, and quite infectious; while his flair for dialogue makes this debut an understated success.' *Telegraph*

'An unusually mature debut from a talented writer.' *Q*

'Essential reading.' *Options*

'This novel is loaded with promise, written with poise, and lives from the inside, with conviction and with the feeling that, inexorably, it will hold you in its mesmerising thrall.' *Scotland on Sunday*

'A wonderfully original, dotty and ultimately romantic first novel.' *Irish Times*

by the same author

INTERESTING FACTS ABOUT THE STATE OF ARIZONA

AUDACITY'S SONG

A Ghost Story

Jeremy Poolman

faber and faber

LONDON · BOSTON

First published in Great Britain in 1998
by Faber and Faber Limited
3 Queen Square London WC1N 3AU

Phototypeset by Intype London Ltd
Printed in England by Clays Ltd, St Ives plc

All rights reserved

© Jeremy Poolman, 1998

Jeremy Poolman is hereby identified as author of this work
in accordance with Section 77 of the Copyright,
Designs and Patents Act 1988.

This book is sold subject to the condition that it shall not,
by the way of trade or otherwise, be lent, resold, hired out or
otherwise circulated without the publisher's prior consent in
any form of binding or cover other than that in which it is
published and without a similar condition including this
condition being imposed on the subsequent purchaser

A CIP record for this book is
available from the British Library

ISBN 0–571–19200–9

2 4 6 8 10 9 7 5 3 1

For Tracy and Joanna, my wonderful beautiful talented sisters; and for Joanne, again, who teaches me how to live.

Acknowledgements

I would like to acknowledge a debt to the following:

The Arts Council of England, for their support during the writing of this book; Beryl Bainbridge, for her kindness; Matthew Bates of the Tessa Sayle Agency, for representing me; Russell Gilchrist, for being my brother; Professor Kaiser Haq, for his generous words; Pepin Jimenez, for his autograph; Emma Platt, for all the work; Steve Wariner, for his voice; and, finally, of course, my families, for their love.

I dwell in a lonely house I know
That vanished many a summer ago.
Robert Frost, 'Ghost House'

She is standing at the window, her back toward me, staring out at the slow-falling snow. I step towards her; she turns. Her hair is like flames in the light. 'Look,' she says. 'Have you seen it?'

'Seen what?' I say.

'The snow,' she says.

Outside, way off, a trucker blasts his horn; inside, in the warm, on the Fairview's dipping bed, we hold each other tight like abandoned survivors on some homeward-bound ship.

But it's not over – we both know this. We both know there is more to come.

We close our eyes. We drift. We sleep.

I ease out of bed in the last light of dusk, creep like a thief to the window. There are lights across the forecourt like birds shot electric in a tree and scratchy music – Elvis, 'I'll Be Home for Christmas' – the thud in my ears of my own heart beating.

She stirs, stretches in the window's other world. 'Billy?' she says. 'What's wrong?'

My breath clouds the glass. 'Promise me something,' I say.

The rustle of bedclothes as she lifts her head. 'Okay,' she says, her voice is full of sleep. 'What?'

'That we'll always be together.'

'Always?' she says.

I turn. 'On this day. You and me. The two of us. Nobody else.'

'Nobody?' she says. She squints in the low light.

'Promise me,' I say.

She pulls back the covers. 'I promise,' she says. She is naked. With a finger tipped blood-red she crosses her heart.

Tuesday

The Girl with Transmitting Teeth

I was thinking tonight of a story the Doctor used to tell about a girl with transmitting teeth. The story, as related to me, goes as follows.

Once upon a time there was a girl who arrived at the Institute with her mother, complaining (the girl not the mother) of voices in her head – and not just any voices, mind, but singing voices, country music, she said, day and night that had gotten so bad that she'd had to quit her job at the plastics plant (not to mention forget about joining the Navy – always her greatest dream) and at night she was quite unable to sleep. It was, she said, driving her as nuts as some folks reckoned she was already (what with her wanting to join the Navy in such dangerous times), and two or three times at least she'd come real close to suicide. Day and night, she said, all she could hear was Vince Gill and Hal Ketchum, and on Sundays the Hossman's selection of Songs from the Archives. She was, she said, in one terrible state, and if he – the Doctor – couldn't help her then all that remained for her were those tracks outside of town and the wheels of the ten forty-one southbound freight.

Well, the Doctor of course – not being a man to shrink from the strange – took up the challenge of curing the girl. At first his attempts at finding a solution were of an entirely physical nature: he looked in her ears and took samples of her various secretions. The results, though, were inconclusive and for a while he was stumped. 'I am stumped,' he said, though this was for him not the end of the matter but rather the beginning – for, from then on, all traditional methods of detection having failed, he felt justified in broadening his scope. So, from the cabinet behind his desk he withdrew a ouija board and, with the help of several of the more balanced of his patients, sought assistance from the Great Beyond. This line, though, also proved fruitless. Seduced by the powers unleashed, a woman from Little Rock claimed in a faltering voice to have been buried before her time, and a man from Nebraska

5

asked if anyone had seen his shoes. Unfortunately, despite these and other connections with the world of the spirits, not a word was said about the girl and her voices and this search for clues was abandoned.

It was later that evening, while the Doctor was listening to his recording of the songs of North American marsh birds, that the terminals were touched in his strange head and the spark of a solution ignited. Slipping off his headphones, he gathered up his portable recording equipment and headed straightway for the poor girl's room. Here, speaking only sufficiently to calm her, he laid her flat on her bed and inserted with care into her mouth a small microphone. Having attached his leads and set his tape to rolling, he waited. At first, despite reproduction through a powerful amp, he heard nothing. Then, as the last dregs of sleep left the girl, he heard something – just a voice at first, distant, all echoes, like a voice heard through a tunnel; then, little by little, a country band kicked in and soon it was really raising hell. There were fiddles and a slide and some back-ups going crazy, and when at last the song was through and the last note had faded, the Hossman cleared his throat and said howdee. 'Folks,' he said through that familiar AM hiss, 'that there was a song called "Circular World" and here's another called "I Got a Flat Though the Road Sure Is Bumpy" – kinda makes ya think, don't it?'

Well the Doctor smiled, though not at the Hossman's talk. He flicked his eyes to the girl. 'Miss,' he said, reaching forward to take the microphone from her mouth, 'though the problem was complex, the solution as ever was simple.'

'Simple?' said the girl. Relief and disbelief were playing tag across her face.

The Doctor stood and crossed to the window. 'The solution,' he said, turning suddenly for emphasis, 'lies in your teeth.'

'My teeth?' said the girl.

'Or, to be precise, it lies within the metal that lies within your teeth. In short, miss, your teeth and the metal that lies within them must at once be removed – if, that is, the reign of the Opry is to come to an end.' The Doctor then gathered his equipment and crossed the room. He paused at the door and turned back to the open-mouthed girl. 'At once,' he repeated and then he was gone.

The girl's teeth were removed three weeks later at the LeBaron Dental Hospital in Amarillo, Texas, and their owner equipped with a false set quite devoid of the powers of radio transmission. As for the girl herself, she became (so the story goes) – on at last being accepted into the Navy – a wireless operator on board the USS *Saratoga*, where presumably she remains to this day.

And the teeth?

The teeth – reconstructed into a set, upper and lower, and mounted on a small block of wood (teak I think) – sit tonight, as you can see, in the palm of my hand, a reminder, as the Doctor said on the day of my leaving the Institute, not only of his own extraordinary powers, but also of the power of music to haunt and beguile.

Twenty-Four Miles from Tulsa

I've been counting the hours left until Christmas and wondering again about Audacity. Sometimes I'm certain she'll come, sometimes I'm certain she won't. Whatever, whether she does or she doesn't, Christmas is coming fast (a hundred something hours and counting I make it), and there are things I must do – get my story straight for one thing – a story which is not going to get told at all if I keep spinning off in all kinds of directions, discussing musical teeth and such like, or Alice and her sudden departure.

So.

My story.

To begin, as they say, at the beginning.

For the record, I was born William James Songhurst, the second of three children, on September 28th 1959. The place I was born was right here on my Uncle Braxton's farm in Creek County which is in the state of Oklahoma, twenty-four miles from the Tulsa city line, which was twenty-four miles too close Uncle Braxton always said, him not holding with cities like Aunt Celeste. Now, to this day, I don't know whether it was the real reason or not, but Aunt Celeste said Uncle Braxton's dislike of cities was on account of his having had his right leg taken clean off at the knee on Aurora Street in 1948 by a man named Tyler who'd come into town that morning with the express purpose of getting himself drunk – a feat which evidently he managed to achieve with some ease by nine o'clock. Just exactly how he came to be cutting off Uncle Braxton's leg I don't know (Aunt Celeste could never bring herself to say but I can guess) – all I do know is the accident happened somehow as the man got arrested and fined thirty-five dollars for being Drunk and Dangerous in Charge of a Motor Vehicle – and besides, there was the other evidence – namely Uncle Braxton's leg from the knee down that he had Mr Feedle from Feedle's Funeral Services put in a cherry box with a hinged top and which one time in a time of fever he arranged to have sent to the Smithsonian Museum in

Washington DC, but which they sent back with a note saying they didn't collect legs no more since they took the leg of General Sickles during the Civil War, even though it was the leg of another war hero which Uncle Braxton was. You know, looking back now, I remember like it was yesterday the arguments Uncle Braxton and my daddy had over that leg (and over pretty much everything else for that matter) – how my daddy said keeping it standing up in the parlor behind the TV wasn't hygenic, and how you could smell it in the summer when the breeze through the house was just right and how it smelled like a pig left to rot in the fields. Even now, after all these years, with Uncle Braxton gone and Aunt Celeste and both Daddy and Mama now too, I can still smell that leg and Daddy's smokes, and sometimes at night when I'm lying in my bed and the TV's flickering in the darkness I swear I can hear that shouting in the yard and the slamming of that old screen door.

But I digress.

As I was saying, I was born the second of three children, the first of whom was Larry and the third of whom was Alice. Alice, had she lived past the forty-five minutes that was given to her on this earth, would today be twenty-eight and I today would have a sister. Though this loss is not one upon which I have generally dwelt, I have to admit that lately it has been playing on my mind some, which I suppose is only human nature. It's human nature I suppose for a person to sometimes think about what might have been – to indulge themselves if you like in fantasies. In my case it's these fantasies regarding Alice that I see now were the cause, at least in part, of my recent troubles and which led – with the inevitability promised by the Doctor – to my situation as it stands today.

But again I digress. Chronology, the Doctor says, is important. If things in the telling are to make any sense they must, he says, be placed in the right order. Only Chinamen, he says, are equipped to read backwards; Americans must look straight ahead. We are, he says, a straightforward-in-essence people, a people verging at times – due to the nature of our history – on the blinkered, a claim for which, as far as evidence is concerned, you only, he says, have to look as far as that great American fool and hero Charlie Lindbergh, though he never did explain exactly why.

Anyhow.

Back to my life.

First, though, a final word about the Doctor and that girl. As I sit here tonight, I am struck again and again by the image of those tracks outside of town. Sitting here, trying to recall what I know of the past, I swear sometimes – just for the briefest of moments – that I can almost feel the cool of their metal through my shirt, almost hear in the silence the whistle of that freight as it grows ever nearer and ever more distinct.

But of course this is all just delusion – just the result of too much time spent alone. Surely the past recalled can never hurt again – surely what's done really is done?

11.53

The Tour Starts Here

That rain sweeping down, bright in the shaft of the parking-lot lights, the sickness of losing in my stomach: this now – this and Audacity, the growl of her Firebird growing faint – my memory tonight of that day. Tonight as ever that day is close, three months like three seconds, and tonight as ever there is nothing I can do. I call out, but these walls take my words; I search for her face, but the night blinds my eyes.

'You're joking, right?'

How absurd it seems now, that mocking in my voice. Why could I not have just smiled? A smile costs nothing and can gain so much. But no. My voice rising sharp against the rhythm of the band, the words came spitting out. 'You're joking, right?' I said, though I knew in my heart in that moment of speaking it was no joke, 'This is some kind of sick joke, right?'

Uh-uh. She shook her head, looked down, up sharp. 'So what are you saying?' she said, her voice like a whisper against Bitter Pete's guitar. Thinking of nothing, I just shook my head, turned away. Out front in the darkness a hall full of faces. I turned back; hers was gone. Is gone still.

And then?

Then I'm driving, turning this way and that, my hands on the wheel gripping tight. The darkness of an underpass, the glare of Amarillo's lights and I'm traveling fast, nothing in my head but her sweet shaming face. *So what are you saying?*: again and again her words come back to me and I push that thing faster, searching the sidewalks for her shape, until the city bleeds away and the night and the country wrap their arms around me, squeezing me, and I drift to a stop on the shoulder.

Well, aren't you pleased? Sitting there, door open, my face bathed cool in the courtesy light, her words were like some echo from a dream, and from the darkness beyond solemn faces appeared, nodded, raised a hand then spun away – Mama, Daddy, that truck-driving man: all loomed, fell back, came again, faces twisted, urgent, but in the end helpless, too far away when it mattered to be heard. I leaned forward, staring hard, caught the eyes of Chief Yellowhammer and the curl of his smile, then he too was gone and the darkness rolled over, pouring in through the open door, and in time I slept and dreamed. In my dream I was standing in back of Mama's gas station, one foot either side of the state line, when suddenly that line split apart, wider and wider. I looked down, to the sparkle of water in the depths of some canyon, and then I was falling, the moving air smooth as hands on my cheeks, then gasping for breath as the water rose above me, and then I was still like I was sleeping but watching myself sleeping, and then there was nothing.

I woke to the sound of a horn. I lifted my head. It stopped. I squinted in the harsh morning light. My mouth was dusty, my limbs filled with sleep. I pushed myself out of the car, stood up.

'Howdee,' said a voice.

I turned.

Leaning back against the car, hands in his pockets and an Orioles baseball cap pulled low across his brow, was a young man – a kid really – maybe thirteen, maybe fourteen, his clothes dusty like he'd just quit burrowing like some animal in the dirt – his hair, too – and barefoot, his feet as brown as some Indian's. He had his head cocked sly to one side, was watching me from beneath the peak of his cap like he was studying some creature in a cage.

'Reckoned you for deeed,' he said.

'Who are you?' I said.

He shrugged, looked away, out across the scrub. I followed his gaze. Way in the distance was a small group of buildings that seemed unattached to the highway by a road. They seemed to shimmer despite the cold air.

'It don't matter,' said the boy.

'What?' I said.

He turned back. 'Who I am. It don't matter.' He cocked his head again, the smile crept back. 'You that singer?' he said. 'I's seen you in Mama's magazine, ain't I?'

'Maybe,' I said. My head was pounding with the night and too much thinking. 'Look,' I said, 'did you see a Firebird pass by here?'

The boy shook his head, he was grinning now. 'You know Mama

says you and that Audacity's like cheese and chalk. Says it's oil and water when you two get together.' He shrugged then. 'Course,' he said, glancing a second over his shoulder as if he feared being overheard, 'Mama don't know nothin'. She says the President's got his hand in some pie or other – and you know what she says about school? Satan's seat of evil, she says. Did you know I ain't never been to school since I don't know when? Say, where you goin', mister? You goin' after that Firebird?'

I shifted the stick back to park. 'You *saw* her?' I said.

The boy had his face now close to mine. His teeth when he smiled were a startling white. 'Sure I saw her,' he said, frowning suddenly like I'd asked him the dumbest question in the world.

'Which way?' I said.

The boy pushed up, stepped away from the car, started fumbling in his pockets.

'Look, I'm sorry,' I said. 'It's just – '

The boy stopped his fumbling then, looked up. 'Sorry?' he said.

'I didn't mean – '

And it was then, slowly, watching it all the while like he was watching some living thing that might just scoot away, he pulled out the contents of his pocket. It was smooth and oval-shaped, the color of cream. He stepped back towards the car, his palm out-stretched. 'Say howdee,' he said, and with his free hand he turned the thing around, until sitting grinning on his palm was the clean-picked skull of a child.

'Jesus Christ,' I said. 'What the hell is that?'

The boy shrugged. 'Just a skull,' he said and he turned to walk away. He took a few steps, paused, turned back. Then, with his free hand, he lifted the skull and shook it. For a moment there was silence – perhaps the faintest clicking and whirring. Then, with the boy grinning suddenly, the skull started singing 'God Bless America' in a tiny tinny voice. 'Sure is purdy, huh?' he said.

I nodded, shifted the stick to drive. As I drove away I glanced in the mirror. Through the dust from my wheels I could see the boy standing, the skull in one hand, the other hand raised in a wave. In a second he was gone, dipping down beneath the rise. I turned on the radio, then turned it off. I gripped the wheel tight, drove on.

12.00

Bells and Bones

The Sayreville bells toll the hour then are quiet. Everything here is quiet. No sound here now but the beating of my heart disturbs the silence. Nothing but memory lives in this night world. I close my eyes. The past lives.

My daddy smiling: this is what I see, then circles in the water as a body cuts the surface. He turns slow, revolving, arms outstretched and fingers splayed as if for balance. Down and down he goes, into unseen depths. He struggles, settles, is still.

Time passes.

I open my eyes, squint at the glow of my watch. Bones. He is nothing now but bones. I lift my arm, place finger and thumb on my pounding temples. *Take care of your mama, y'hear?* I am nodding, nodding, a boy of thirty-five. I feel the touch of his rough calloused hands. I see his dust rise as the time ticks by and is gone, hear the echo of his pick-up in the trees.

Wednesday

7.10

I'm Starting to Worry

I'm starting to worry these days about things that have never worried me before. This development in itself I find worrying.

Take last night for example.

Last night, I was lying in bed just trying to think of nothing – just trying to get some sleep – when clean out of nowhere the budget deficit crept into my mind. Well I tried to shut it out, tried to ignore it in the hopes that it might go away, but I could not and it would not. It just sat there in the darkness, squatting on my chest like it was aiming to squeeze all the life from my body and do to me in miniature just exactly what it's been doing on a larger scale to the American economy. No matter which way I turned, it was still there pushing down on me, dominating my thoughts and planting into my mind solutions to the problem the craziness of which only now, in the pale light of day, am I becoming aware. Of course I know now that just printing a whole heap more money and sending it off in suitcases to Tokyo or wherever is some way from sound economics – I know this now, but I didn't know it then. Then, in my crazy night world, it was as brilliant a solution as it was an obvious one, and I couldn't for the life of me figure out why nobody had thought of it before. Of course even in time the deficit, enormous and crippling as it is, got lost in the shadow of other larger worries as my mind moved on, getting ever deeper and deeper, further away with every minute from that clear-conscience sleeping of a child.

Of these other worries, the biggest and most pressing was and is the problem of what to do about Stig's barn. Stig's barn has been a disaster just waiting to happen for some days now – ever since the storm that blew the top off the stack (another worry) and ripped out the fenceposts that ran along the highway and tossed them into the air like they were nothing but a handful of toothpicks. Since then it's just been a matter of time until the whole thing comes crashing down – unless, that is, I manage to do something about it and real soon. But what? Am I a carpenter? Am I even a farmer? No, sir. What I am (or maybe was, it's hard to tell) is a musician, which is not so useful a thing to be in a situation like this – except of course in the middle of the night. In the middle of the night, of course, a musician is just exactly what is needed to solve this or any problem. A person like me just lies in the darkness and lets the problems come on, and then, sure enough, though it may take some time – hours sometimes of scrutinizing shadows – sooner or later he's got the answer.

Like last night.

No sooner had I solved the problem of the deficit, than my attention was turned to the barn. A problem? Not for long, for soon I had the solution. All I had to do was get on that telephone and call up Bubba at the store and he'd come over in that dirty red pick-up of his and fix it. Last night it was as simple as that – and it would be still if it weren't for the fact that this house no longer has a working telephone. It's been out since I arrived here from the Institute nearly two weeks ago now. Twice in that time I've picked it up, forgetting, and dialed the phone company, and twice of course there's been nothing but silence on the line – just the sound of my breathing in the hall. I should go into town I know, use Bubba's phone to get connected again, and maybe I will later. First, though, there's breakfast to be had and my daily walk (more in hope than in expectation) up to the mailbox on the highway.

7.25

Praying for Louie

It occurred to me just now while I was eating my breakfast (eggs again, of course, plus a few beans left over from last night), that if Louie hadn't died during that Amarillo gig then I'd probably not have been so on edge and – as a consequence – I'd maybe not have said what I said to Audacity and maybe not, then, found myself cruising so hopeless next morning through that glaring Texas sun, just trying to forget about everything, just trying to drive, and I maybe wouldn't have been so jumpy when my mobile sang out from the pocket of my coat. But he did die, and I did say those things, and I did jump like crazy at the sound of that phone – so much in fact that I had to pull over to take the call.

'Audacity?' I said.

'Billy?'

Well even now I can feel my heart dipping. 'Hey, Carl,' I said.

'You heard?' he said.

'Heard what?' I said.

'Then you ain't heard?'

'Heard what?'

For a moment then there was nothing – just static on the line, the fading power of a battery.

'Carl?' I said.

'Where are you?' he said.

'Where am I?' I looked around. It was just Texas scrub. 'I don't know,' I said. 'Why?'

'You better come by,' he said.

'Why?' I said.

The connection flickered, died. I dialed Carl's number. Nothing. I waited a minute, dialed again. Silence. I sat still a moment, let my eyes close. I was feeling so weary that I swear I could have slept for a week. I tossed the phone into the back and started the engine.

It was only maybe fifteen miles to the Oklahoma line, but those fifteen miles were some of the longest miles I've ever driven. With every mile that passed I couldn't help thinking the worst – that Carl Cooper knew something, that something had happened to Audacity – and the worst – with every mile – just kept getting worse until it was real real bad.

Now, looking back on it, I suppose I should have known that Larry would be at the bottom of things – what with Larry pretty much always being at the bottom of things when things aren't going as they should – but at the time I was just too tired and too wound up to think straight. All I kept thinking was something had happened to Audacity – something bad – that maybe she'd meant what she'd said about ending things, and the more I thought about it the more I knew I had to get to Carl real fast, which accounts for the speed I was doing past that Texas state trooper and the wailing that that speeding attracted.

'PULL OVER!' barked a voice through a hailer.

I lifted my foot off the gas.

'I SAID PULL OVER!'

I pulled on to the shoulder and drew to a stop. The trooper pulled up behind me. I watched him get out of his car. He was a tall thin man – even taller and thinner when he put on his hat. He paused, squinting through his shades at my plates, then moved towards me real casual-like but wary too.

He tapped on my window, which I lowered.

'Outta state?' he said.

'Look, Officer – ' I said.

'You got a license?'

'It's a kind of emergency – '

'I said you got a license?'

I found my wallet. He studied my license. 'You him?' he said, and I thought at once of the boy with the skull. 'You that Willy Songhurst?'

'Billy,' I said. 'Look – '

'You his brother then?'

I shook my head.

He returned the license. 'Too bad,' he said. 'The wife kinda likes him. Course she likes all that country shit. You traveling far?'

I sat myself up. 'That what I've been trying to tell you,' I said.

''Cause you sure is traveling fast. You know what you was doing?'

'Doing?' I said.

'Miles-per-hour-wise. Eighty-three. I clocked you. Say, you know what the limit is in Texas?'

Yes, I said, I knew what the limit was in Texas. Same as Oklahoma.

'That's right,' he said. He was smiling. He stepped back, placed a hand on his holster, suggested I step out of the car.

'But – ' I said.

He flicked off the safety with his thumb.

I got out of the car.

He told me to turn around.

'What?' I said.

'I said turn around. Place your hands against the car.'

'Look,' I said, 'Officer. You don't understand – ' and I was just getting ready to tell him exactly what it was he didn't understand – how things by then were getting urgent – when he pulled out his pistol and cocked it.

'Now,' he said. 'You was sayin'?'

I turned around.

'Better,' he said. A hand pushed me forward, hard against the car. 'Now,' he said, 'you carrying a firearm?'

I shook my head.

'You sure now?'

Maybe it was the no-sleeping or the driving or something, but suddenly my head felt as heavy as a boulder.

'I said you sure now?'

'I'm sure,' I said. My voice seemed muffled like I was listening to it through a body of water, and when I spread my legs as he told me and felt hands running up them and over my arms, my arms and my legs and the lids of my eyes felt so damned heavy that I just let my eyes close for a second. When I opened them my head was lying flat on the roof of the car.

' . . . trunk,' a voice was saying.

'What?' I said. I lifted my head, things were shifting.

'I said open the trunk.'

'The trunk? But, Officer – '

'Yeah,' he said. 'The trunk.' He regripped his pistol.

'Okay,' I said, 'okay.' Then, slowly, like I was pushing my legs through a swamp, I made my way around the car. The sky overhead was bright and glaring off the chrome. I opened the trunk.

'Oh, Jesus,' said the officer. He pulled out a handkerchief, held it over his nose. 'What the hell's that?'

I leaned a little forward, peered into the gloom. 'That's Louie,' I said.

'Louie?'

'Uh-huh.'

The officer leaned forward, took a look. 'You mean that's . . . *the* Louie?'

'Yes,' I said. I had to get going.

'You mean – '

My head was pounding now, getting worse with every minute.

'Jesus,' said the officer, lowering his handkerchief, 'Jesus Christ.'

'Look,' I said, 'Officer – ' and I put my hand on the trunk lid aiming to close it – and I would have closed it – would have been halfway to Carl and the Slicknickle Family Restaurant by now – if that officer hadn't leaned forward into the gloom and laid a hand on Louie's still breast.

'How?' he said softly.

'What?' I said.

There were stars in my eyes now, gathering then dispersing like busted constellations.

The officer turned, peeled off his shades. There were tears suddenly in the tall man's eyes. 'The end,' he said, 'when it came. It was peaceful, wasn't it? I mean he didn't suffer none – did he?'

Jesus Christ.

'Well he didn't – did he?'

I shook my head. 'No,' I heard myself saying, and for a moment I thought, I'm dreaming all this, but then a hand on my arm told me otherwise.

'Thank God,' said the officer – LaDrupe from his name badge – 'Thank the merciful Lord'; then, before I knew what was happening, he was down on his knees right there on the roadside in the middle of nowhere, his head lowered in meek supplication and his hands clasped together in an attitude of prayer. 'Let us pray,' he said.

'What?' I said. '*Here?*' At which, for the second time that morning, he pulled out his pistol and aimed that thing right at me.

'I said pray, boy,' he said.

'Are you serious?' I said.

He cocked that hammer. He was serious alright.

It was gone eleven when we finally got through praying and I finally got going, the prayers for Louie still ringing in my ears as I turned down the visors and headed east. That Texas sun was by then just about overhead, rippling the road like the road was melting, but that heat meant nothing – nothing meant nothing – 'cause all I could think was I'm gonna be too late, and all I could picture was Audacity Vine, truly the love of my life, her body growing cool after some terrible accident, her clothes in disarray, while I'd been on my knees at the edge of an Interstate praying for the soul of a goose.

Climbing the Glories

Two letters today, neither of course from Audacity. I suppose I shouldn't be disappointed, though every morning of course I am. That's hope for you or foolishness I suppose. I mean after all that's happened between us I couldn't honestly expect any kind of communication from her – except perhaps a lawyer's letter – and against that there's the fact that nobody knows I'm here. They will soon enough I guess (particularly if I take that phone trip into town); for now, though, I'm pretty much alone. For now at least I have no one to regard but myself.

Anyhow.

Back to the phone.

It occurred to me during my walk up to the highway this morning that there's something real symmetrical in the fact of this house being probably the first in the county to get itself cut off, seeing as how it was this house (according to Uncle Braxton) that was the first to get itself connected in the first place. I know the Lord works in mysterious ways His wonders to perform – well, likewise the phone company it seems. Which is not to say I'm in any way likening one to the other, although they both do sometimes seem to act in a real high-handed not to say sometimes downright stupid way.

For example, the first of these letters.

Dear Resident, it says, *We see from our records that the invoice sent to you on July 7th requesting a check in the sum of $47.50 to cover the cost of disconnection has received no reply. We would be grateful therefore if you would let us have the above sum by return. Should you fail to do so I have to warn you that steps will be taken to recover the sum outstanding. Yours faithfully, R. Gilchrist, Customer Liaison.* Steps? What will they do – cut me off? (Which reminds me of the story of the soldier in Vietnam who was caught stealing money from the pockets of American corpses. 'So what you gonna do?' he asked the officer presiding at his court martial, 'Send me to Vietnam?') Anyway, right now typical is how this madness seems. These days, it seems the condemned man must pay for his executioner's ammunition, the trampled little man for the privilege of his trampling. Sometimes these days it's like the whole notion of society has just gone all to hell, and sometimes lately it's amazing to me that we all live as long as we do, what with all of us being dominated by the ways of commerce, and the ways of commerce being the way they are. And it's not just commerce. Sometimes it's just everything that seems lost in chaos, and like sooner or later it's just all gonna fall.

But hey. Back to those letters.

Letter number two came in a buff-colored envelope, my daddy's name – Mr Glenn G. Songhurst – peering out through a transparent window. For a moment I just stood there by the highway staring down at it, squinting through my billowing breath, unable for the life of me to think who'd be writing to such a dead man. I turned it over. On the back, printed in hard black letters, it said DEPART-MENT OF CORRECTIONS, and I knew at once what that meant.

Larry.

I turned it back, stared again at the name, and I was just getting up the will to open it when the sound of a car horn split the air, nearly stopping my heart right there in my chest. The sound of gravel, then the hiss of damp brakes and I turned. I squinted in the glare off the windshield as the fender of a Pontiac gently nudged my knee. A window buzzed down, a balding head appeared. 'Well, shoot, Billy-Boy,' said a voice I knew but have not heard for years, 'I thought you was you and you is!'

Though now heavenside of seventy, I can tell you Checker Noose-felt seems as large today as ever he did when I was a child and he was an officer – a sheriff's deputy – whose beat was Creek County here in central Oklahoma. Today – just as then – to see him squeezed behind the wheel, his great belly spilling over, is to see the unlikely, and to see him heave and wrestle his way out of that vehicle and somehow into a standing position is to witness one of life's smaller miracles. To say – even today, when eyes once so deep are now the palest of blues and hands once so steady now a study in shakes – that Checker Noosefelt is large is to say that Johnny Cash is the Man in Mid-Grey or that Geraldo is a person with a thing or two to say. Even today, at past seventy, he's large enough still with large enough hands to make you check your own for damage after shaking one in greeting – which was precisely what I was doing this morning, kneading the life back into my right hand with the thumb and fingers of my left – when, on the heels of a question about all the places I must have been in the last nearly twenty years, as if suddenly remembering something he rushed off his hat and begged me in a low tone for forgiveness.

'What for?' I said.

His jowls flushed with guilt, Checker Noosefelt slid cowed eyes to his Pontiac then back to meet mine. 'For blowin' my horn,' he said low. He stepped forward; I stepped back, fearing the great bear's crushing embrace. He looked about him as if suspecting watching eyes. 'On a Sunday,' he whispered.

'Oh I see,' I said, though I didn't see at all.

He nodded gravely. It was, he said, against the law.

'It is?' I said.

He flicked his eyes up the highway. As he turned back, a glinting sixteen-wheeler appeared on the brow in the distance, the noise of its engine hanging muffled in the moist air. 'Uh-huh,' he said, nodding, as if reminding himself, 'no horns on a Sunday. It's the law.' Again he edged forward; again I edged back. His voice again when he spoke was a whisper – just a hiss like the whisper of a child in the dark. 'Do you think – ' he started, pausing then like he was struggling with conscience or something. 'Do you think – do you think anybody heard?'

I studied the old boy's face. He had suddenly all the worries of the world in his eyes.

'Well do you?' he said.

I shook my head and it came to me then that I'd been wrong: sure he was as large as ever he had been – no doubt about that – but that didn't mean the years hadn't taken their toll. Where once, then, he'd seemed so solid, so eye to eye with the world, he now had about him an old man's indecision, an old man's crippling fear of the future. I tried to raise a smile to reassure him.

'You think?' he said. Behind him, the truck was getting nearer, its wheels spitting stones on the shoulder.

'We'd better step back,' I said.

'What's that?' said Checker.

I took his bear's arm and led him across the verge and down a shallow dip. 'Billy?' he said, and then he said something more that was lost in the screaming of the truck. In a moment then the truck was gone (I waited for the blast of a horn but – it being a Sunday – it never came), haring off down the highway, and the silence returned then, settled still on the land.

'You okay?' I said.

Checker Noosefelt was squinting hard across the highway, his straining eyes fixed on something far off. I followed his gaze, but could see nothing but the silos tiny and distant and pale blue against the stark winter sky.

I opened my mouth to speak, but something stopped me. I looked again, and in that moment of looking I knew what it was that the old man could see. A figure, a child, climbing the furthest silo.

'Jesus Christ,' he said, he was breathing hard like a bull now, steam pouring from his nostrils. 'Ain't that brother of yours never gonna learn?'

I stared hard at the silo.

'Hell, didn't I tell your daddy to whup that boy good before somebody else gets to doin' it?'

I nodded. It was true: thirty years ago now he'd said such a thing, but my daddy never had been one for whupping. Instead he'd made Larry sweep the yard.

Checker Noosefelt shook his head, turned to me. 'Your daddy home, son?' he said. 'I gotta talk to that man – '

I shook my head. I could see again from the window of our room Larry dragging that brush across the yard's uneven surface, hear again the whisper of its bristles in the dust. For a moment the scene was as clear now as it had been then, the cool of the window against my cheek as cool and real as the sharp winter air. I closed my eyes tight. When I opened them the scene had fled along with the years.

'Son?' said Checker Noosefelt. 'Are you listenin' to me?'

'Sure,' I said. So much now has fled and so fast that sometimes it seems scarcely anything remains.

'Well I was askin' you a question.'

'I know.'

'Well?'

I turned sharp. 'Look,' I said, and I wanted to say for God's sake let it go, but something stopped me – perhaps the fear of raising a person too fast from too deep. Instead I turned away.

'Son?'

'Nothing,' I said. I pointed to the silos. 'Can you really see somebody?'

He squinted.

'Checker?'

'Well – '

'Come on,' I said. I touched his arm. 'You okay?'

Checker's stare was losing edge, his face twitching with the effort of seeing. 'Well – ' he said, a stammer creeping in, 'I-I don't know, son – '

I shook my head. Of course he's not there, I wanted to say, how could he be?

Suddenly Checker's shoulders lost their line as the weight of years came flooding back. He raised a gnarled hand to his eyes and covered them. 'Oh, Lord,' he said. 'I coulda sworn – ' There was something then – a lost something – in his voice.

I looked away, across the frozen fields to the silos. For a moment in the distance there were voices – an echo of an echo – then there was nothing, just the silos – Sayreville's Glories – sitting still, blind, unmoved.

I walked slowly back down the track to the house, pausing at the barn. From there, looking back up to the highway, I could see Checker Noosefelt standing by his car, his great bulk dark against the frozen fields. He half raised a hand; I half raised mine. Then he turned, moved heavily around the car and heaved himself in. In a moment came the distant cough of a car starting up. I watched it moving away, climb slow like a tired old bear up the road. Then it was gone, lost in the pencil trees.

That was an hour ago now. Since then I've been standing here by the barn, turning these letters over and over in my hands and wondering if it's true when people say that everything changes, everything moves on, and that all we need do is await the passage of time.

8.10

I've Just Discovered Something

I've just discovered that I'm becoming – much to my surprise – a
man of routines. After fifteen years of no routines but the routine
of the road I can tell you this is strange and a little unnerving.
Fifteen years of a new and unfamiliar home every night, of doors
that won't shut and some that won't open, of some places so cold
you can see your breath freezing and others so hot you can't move
for nearly dying, is something you get used to and becomes who
you are. But just then, just when you think you know yourself, one
thing changes and everything changes, and suddenly you're not
who you thought you were at all. I mean I look at myself now and
for sure I really don't recognize myself. I smile at myself in Aunt
Celeste's old mirror and it's a stranger smiling back. I close my
eyes tight, open them, and there he is staring back. Some days we
stare at each other for hours, him and me, neither one of us wanting
to be the first to speak. And some days – like today – it's not just
speaking, but moving too. I twitch, he twitches; I bluff to move, he
bluffs to move. Only difference is his clock's going backwards while
mine, of course, is moving on and on, chipping away at the hours
remaining.

Which brings me to Christmas, and in particular the problem of
what to do about Larry. Which is this. In his letter to my daddy,
the Governor of the Elk City Penitentiary mentions the problem of
visiting hours, adding then that for the prison's current state of calm
to continue 'the prisoners must on no account be made to feel
isolated during this, the festive season'. He goes on to say that the
Friends of the Pen have kindly donated three dozen turkeys
(complete with all the trimmings), and that these (to be followed
by a selection of seasonal sweets) will form the centerpiece of this
year's celebration. 'In addition,' he writes, 'following the conclusion
of the Elk City Players' production of *The Sound of Music*, there will
commence an hour or so of amusements.' All of which would be
fine of course were it not for the Governor's concluding paragraph,

during which he makes mention of guests. Each prisoner, it seems, is to be allowed one family guest, which, in Larry's case, would be me, my being his only living relative. Which of course is my problem: how to be in two places at once? Knowing Larry as I do I know for certain that if he were the only inmate without a guest then it'd surely affect him real bad and lead, I wouldn't be at all surprised, to some kind of trouble and his further putting back his chances of parole, which – even as it stands at the moment – could not be said to be good, the judge having said that, due to his obvious outstanding stupidity and consequent danger to the safety of the public, he should not be released before the Man in the Moon declares himself a Democrat. So – that all being the case – what should I do? If I stay here, Larry goes nuts; if I go, what if Audacity shows up after all? I tell you, right now it's a problem for which I can see no solution, and believe me I've been looking. I've even considered flipping a coin – heads Larry, tails Audacity – but in the end this really seems no solution for a rational man. Chance, after all, is okay for games, but this is my life and, Jesus, surely my life is more than a game?

8.25

The Tammy Wynette World and All Known Planets Appreciation Society

These days, all that remains of the once-prosperous west Oklahoma town of Boom! is the Slicknickle Family Restaurant (Home of the 'Slicknickle Six-Bun') and a squat breeze-block and tin building known to all as Carl's Country Cabin. A radio station dedicated exclusively to the life and works of Miss Tammy Wynette, the cabin has a staff of one (Carl) and takes just one commercial. It was this commercial:

> *Come to Boom!*
> *Oh, come to Boom!*
> *There's always room*
> *So come back soon!*

that was jangling from my radio as I pulled up in that dirt those three months ago now in the shade of the restaurant.

I cut the engine and sat a moment. The day was burning hot now and my head was banging hard, and I was just stepping out, heading for the cabin and some answers, when a voice I recognized from high up behind me declared to the world that Billy Songhurst was a liar.

I kept walking.

'Well!' said the voice. 'You hearing me, mister?'

Without stopping, without breaking my stride, I said, 'I hear you, Mrs Cooper.'

'Well then?'

I banged on the cabin door.

'Carl?'

'He ain't there, mister,' said Mrs Cooper.

I banged, called again.

Mrs Cooper snorted. 'Ain't you hearing me, liar-boy?'

I turned, squinted into the sun. Mrs Cooper – Carl's mama and one of only three permanent residents of Boom! – was standing in her nightdress at the window above the restaurant. Mrs Cooper, everyone knew, had not been the same since the death of her husband, and everyone knew you had to tread wary. 'Would you know where he is?' I said. It was tough to see. 'Mrs Cooper?'

'What?'

'Carl – would you know where he is?'

'Who?'

I sighed. In my mind's eye Audacity was starting up that Firebird again, gunning the engine and spinning the wheels. 'Carl, Mrs Cooper,' I said, 'your son. Have you seen him? It's real urgent, Mrs Cooper – '

'Who's asking?'

'Mrs Cooper?'

'I said who's asking?'

'It's me, Mrs Cooper,' I said. 'Billy. Billy Songhurst.'

'Billy Songhurst?'

'That's right, Mrs Cooper. Me and Carl was in school together – '

'You mean Billy *Liar* Songhurst?'

'What?'

Mrs Cooper gripped the windowsill, leaning out. Her hair was wild and grey, her face white but roughly rouged. Within her night-dress, her body was just skin and bone, her breasts hanging down like socks filled with sand.

A bullet of spit hit the hood of my car.

'Mrs Cooper?'

'I know you,' she said; there was a leer in her voice and dribble on her chin. She leaned forward further still, until it seemed certain she'd fall. 'I heard you,' she hissed. 'On that radio. All smootchie and kootchie – '

Well I sighed. First the skull boy, then that Texas state trooper, then Carl, now this. 'Now, come on, Mrs Cooper,' I said. 'It's just a song. It don't mean nothing – '

'Singing about how you luuurve me – '

'Jesus, Mrs Cooper,' I said, 'you better be careful now – '

Another spit bullet, this as hard as a walnut, hit the dust at my feet. I stepped back.

'Mrs Cooper! Now come on – '

'Liar!'

'You're gonna fall, Mrs Cooper – '

'Calling me honey!'

'Mrs Cooper – '

And then suddenly, out of nowhere, a shot split the air and I ducked. When I looked up, the window was empty – just curtains. I squinted through the sun. 'Mrs Cooper?' I said. 'Are you okay?'

'Hey, Billy,' said a voice from the highway. I turned. 'You looking for me, Billy-Boy?'

Stepping out of the sun, Phoebe Bates, former Under-Twelves Texas State Pistol Shooting Champion (Disabled) blew on her weapon and returned it to its holster. I closed my eyes, drew a long deep breath. 'Phoebe,' I said, so weary suddenly that I knew for sure I might drop at any second if I didn't get some rest and real soon.

'You okay, Billy-Boy?' said a voice drifting off.

I nodded, felt everything shifting. I opened my eyes. For a second everything was dark then light, then there was swirling and voices, then nothing.

When I opened my eyes, I was sitting in a booth in the diner, my head resting heavy on my arms, Phoebe standing over me and frowning. 'Billy?' she was saying, shaking my shoulder, 'Are you alright? Can you hear me?'

I rubbed my eyes, squinted at Phoebe as she slipped into the booth. She settled her withered left arm on the table. 'You should eat,' she said. 'Get something inside you. You want eggs? We got eggs today – '

I felt myself shrugging, heard myself asking for Carl.

Phoebe shook her head. 'Had to go out,' she said.

'Out?'

'Had something to do.'

'Do? What?' My voice sounded distant, muffled like a voice heard through a wall.

Phoebe shrugged, said he looked worried.

'Worried?'

Said he just put on some tapes and took off.

Suddenly I could feel my heart thumping. From way off, it seemed, I heard Audacity's name.

34

'Audacity?' I said. 'She's *here*?'

'Was,' said Phoebe, then she said something about Amarillo –

'When?' I said. My mind was racing. Phoebe glanced through the window, away down the road. The road was rippling in the heat, the heat rising like it was melting the sky. She shrugged, said maybe two hours.

'Two hours?'

'Maybe more. She did leave a message though,' she said.

'A message? What message?'

Very slowly, Phoebe hitched up her left hand toward me, second finger pointing to the ceiling, like so. Then she gave a big shrug and a smile she was smiling still when I started that engine and let that thing rave.

I suppose, looking back, it was either fortune or fate that, an hour or so later, had me passing Carl Cooper on that road heading east. Whatever it was, I was sure giving thanks to God as I stood on those brakes, backed up. In the mirror, I could see Carl backing too. In a second he was alongside. In another I could hear myself shouting.

Carl Cooper was shaking his head. A heavy man prone to sweating, his jowls were glistening, his expression one of gloom. 'Lost her,' he was saying.

'Lost her?' I said.

'Uh-huh,' said Carl. He could scarcely meet my eye. Neither could he when I asked him if she'd said where she was headed. Instead he just shook his heavy head.

'She didn't say anything?' I said.

'Uh-uh,' said Carl, but then he said, 'But – ' and I knew in that moment that something was terribly wrong. I swallowed hard, heard the click in my throat. 'Well?' I said. 'Well?'

Carl Cooper cast his eyes down, eased them up. 'Phoebe didn't tell you then?' he said.

A dagger speared my heart.

'About Larry?'

'Larry?' I said. 'What's Larry got to do with anything?'

It was then that Carl Cooper, Life President of the Tammy Wynette World and All Known Planets Appreciation Society, drew a sweating chubby hand across his face and told me about Larry and his latest bid for stardom in the Being the Biggest Idiot in the Midwest stakes.

'He what?' I said. But then I thought, Audacity, and I grabbed the Life President by his shirt, drew him forward. 'Which way?' I said, my voice screeching like a maniac's. 'For Christ's sakes which way?'

'You mean Larry?' he said, eyes bugging, sweat streaming.

'Uh-uh,' I said, and he seemed to understand, for, released from my grip, he thrust a fat and shaking finger heading east towards Tulsa and all points beyond. I jammed in the shift, revved the engine. 'What?' I called out above the noise – Carl was trying to say something.

'I SAID HAVE YOU GOT A MESSAGE IF HE CALLS?'

'MESSAGE?' I shouted.

'FOR LARRY – '

'UH-HUH,' I said, and I lifted my right hand, second finger extended. Then, with Carl's startled look hanging still in the air, I turned that thing around, stuck my foot to the floor and just let her go.

10.00

Mysterious Ways

According to Mama's old dictionary, chance is 'the unknown and unpredictable element that causes an event to result in a certain way rather than another'. Which means, I suppose, that there's just no telling which things – amongst all the things that happen to you – will be the things that in the end are really gonna matter. It's this not knowing, I suppose, that frightens some people and makes them look to God in the hopes that at least He's got some kind of clue – that there's some kind of plan going on – and that in the end it'll all be making some perfect kind of sense and add up to something that matters. On the other hand, of course, there's people that believe in fate or karma or some such thing – in other words they believe it's all already happened and there's nothing we can do about it except follow the path that's already mapped out.

Me?

Well I just don't know. Sometimes I'm thinking God and that whole Divine Purpose thing (meeting Mary Bibles, for example), and sometimes I'm thinking just fate. I mean, on the one hand, it's hard sometimes to believe in fate when it just feels like everything's choices (I turn left, change my mind, turn right, get chased and knocked down by some crazy in a Studebaker), while, on the other, if it's all down to God, then He sure does have a way with His planning sometimes that I believe could make even Jesus Christ Himself raise His eyebrows.

For example?

Well, Larry for one. I mean sometimes – with the best will in the world – it really is hard to figure – if it is all down to God and His plan – just what exactly the point of it all could possibly be. I mean, for example, what exactly was the point in making him so dumb (not to say so downright unfeeling) that he goes and sells Aunt Celeste's body to science three weeks before she dies and spends the money on a Double Whopper with Extra Cheese – not to mention that whole Elk City thing? I mean Jesus. Some plan. A

37

bank you could understand – even a liquor store. But a state penitentiary? Ain't nobody breaks in to a state penitentiary. People break *out* real regular – do it all the time. But break *in*? Shoot. Ain't *nobody* breaks in. Except my brother Larry. You know sometimes – plan or no plan – it sure does seem like having a brother is the worst thing that can happen to a man.

Okay, okay. I suppose I should say in his defense that maybe it hasn't always been the easiest thing in the world being the brother of Billy Songhurst, Billy Songhurst having been a halfway famous name at least here in Oklahoma. And I guess maybe it's hard having people saying 'So you're the brother' all the time – especially if you've done nothing with your own life except hang out and make trouble and you get to forty-one with nothing to show for it but a famous brother and the clothes you're standing in and an old Chevy pick-up with a stove-in rear fender that only got to be yours on account of a one-legged relative who should have known better but didn't misjudging the flight of a low-flying goose and getting himself struck so hard on the side of the head that I swear he was as dead as every President from Jefferson to Nixon by the time he dropped down in that red Dixie dirt.

Not that I'm excusing nothing, you understand. I'm just saying. Sometimes God's plan for His children gets to be so impossible to make sense of that it makes you start to wonder if there's any plan at all.

And yet, and yet –

Sometimes – even during times when I'm doubting everything, when everything seems so goddamned random – even then, sometimes, there's still – way back someplace – a feeling of patterns I just can't shift. Even then, sometimes, if I look real close, you know I think I can see my daddy's footsteps heading down to that river, and I'll tell you, sometimes, it scares me half to death.

10.23

Mary Bibles

You know, looking back, I see clearly now that Mary Bibles was not only a Flame-Kist waitress but also a tender human being with a heart as big as her Cheeseburger Special. So tender, indeed, was that heart of hers, and so willing her spirit to embrace the troubles of others while having so many of her own, that it shames me now to think of it. It shames me now to think how I turned off that road in the hopes of finding Audacity and sat at that counter thinking only of myself – thinking only I could have worries – and how she sat there beside me, listening to my ranting – how I'd surely killed the person I loved most, as surely as if I'd put Phoebe's pistol to her head and pulled the trigger – and how she laughed at her own small concerns to soothe me as if, in comparison, they were nothing. I'm ashamed now when I think of her laughing at how foolish she'd been to worry so about the overnight loss of the color in the hair (once red, she said, as Vermont in the fall, and of course I thought *Audacity*), and how – next to mine – her troubles were like the troubles of a child. And I can feel now, too, the touch – so light – of her arm on my shoulders as they heaved with the force of my tears. 'There, there,' I can still hear her saying, and how there's nothing so bad that cannot get fixed.

'Fixed?' I said. I looked up. Mary Bibles was smiling, her face blurred through the prism of my tears. 'How can something like this get fixed?'

Mary Bibles took a napkin and dabbed at my cheeks. 'So tell me,' she said, 'this Audacious – '

'Audacity.'

'Okay – Audacity. There must have been a reason she took off like she did – right?' She leaned forward, hung her face before mine. 'Right?'

I shrugged, turned my eyes from hers. For a second she was there again and again I was watching her turn away, disappointment and a sudden hopelessness in her eyes.

'Billy?'

'What?' I flicked my eyes back. 'What is it?' I said, too sharp. 'What are you asking me?'

'Nothing, Billy.' Mary Bibles paused, swept her knees with her palms, looked up. 'It's just – '

'Just what?'

'Well, I've found – '

It's to my shame that I laughed, that I shook my head derisively, and to her pride that she took my derision without resentment.

She pressed on. 'I've found that if you just stay calm – '

'Stay calm?' I shouted. 'Stay calm? How the hell can I stay calm when she's out there God knows where doing God knows what while I'm sitting here with you – ?'

'Well,' said Mary Bibles, an infinite patience in her voice, 'you might find these a little helpful – ' Reaching under her overalls, she eased something out of her pocket.

'Pills?' I said.

She rattled the blue plastic bottle. 'These,' she said softly, 'aren't just pills, Billy Songhurst.' She turned the bottle around in her fingers, held it up to the light as if it were a precious stone of incalculable worth. 'These are the Doctor's special recipe.' She lowered the bottle, held it out on her palm. 'Try one,' she said. 'You'll be amazed – '

I took the bottle, turned it, looked at the label. There was just a name – Dr Ike Rude – and an Oklahoma address. 'What are they?' I said.

'Peace,' said Mary Bibles. 'Acceptance.'

'Acceptance? Acceptance of what?'

'Of the bird in the hand. Of the way things are. Of the proper place for dreams.'

I handed the bottle back. 'I don't think so,' I said.

Mary Bibles set her head to one side and smiled. 'Oh, Billy,' she said, pushing the bottle into my pocket, 'if you could only hear what Doctor Rude says – ' But then, just at that moment, when I was just about to learn what it was exactly that Doctor Rude says, the screen door banged and a low-slung blubber barrel of a man blustered in, all sweat and indignation. 'Well, hot-damn!' he said, whipping off his cap. 'Would you friggin' believe it!'

40

'Hi, Lovely,' said Mary. 'I was just telling Billy here about the Doctor's teachings – '

The big man scowled hard beneath his brows – first at me then at Mary. 'Huh?' he said.

'I said I was just telling Billy here – '

He pulled on his cap, tugged it down. 'Jesus Christ, Mary, I'm standing here having got myself just about killed by some maniac in a Pontiac and you're talking to me about that crank doctor of yours – '

I looked to Mary. She was smiling still. 'Oh, shush now, Lovely,' she said. She turned, winked at me, turned back. 'Billy,' she said, 'I'd like you to meet Lovely Winter. Lovely – this here's Billy Songhurst. He's looking for someone – '

'Oh yeah?' said Lovely Winter. 'Me too. Or I damn well will be. Soon as I get me some coffee I'm outta here – and you know what?'

'What?' I said. He was looking at me.

'When I find that crazy bitch I'm gonna ask her a question. And you know what that question's gonna be?'

I shook my head, aware as I did so of something somewhere falling into place.

Lovely Winter stepped forward, thrust his face so close to mine I thought he was planning to kiss me. 'I'm gonna ask her to tell me if her hair was on fire,' he said, 'And when she tells me it wasn't – when she tells me that red's just as natural and red as my ass – then I'll ask her where it was then – this fire – she was trying to put out by driving so goddamned fast. And then you know what?'

'Jesus Christ,' I said.

'Huh?' said the big man.

My heart suddenly was racing. I stood up. *Maniac in a Pontiac.*

'You okay, honey?' said Mary. 'You look awful pale – '

'This woman,' I said. 'Red hair, you say? Driving a Firebird?'

Lovely Winter frowned. 'Yeah – so?'

I took a deep breath, a second, a third. 'Okay,' I said, and I told myself to stay calm. 'This woman. Did you see which way she was headed?'

Lovely Winter shrugged, looked to Mary, back to me. 'Sure I did,' he said. 'What's it to you?'

'And?' I said.

'And what?'

'And it was – the way? East? West?'

'East,' said Lovely Winter. 'Arkansas. Like some goddamn freight train.' He edged forward. 'Say, she a friend of yours?' He turned to follow me, there was menace suddenly in his voice. 'Say, where you goin', mister?' he said. He thrust out a hand, caught my sleeve. I pulled away, stepped out into the heat. Behind me the screen door banged, then banged again. Walking towards the pick-up, I heard footsteps behind me.

'Say, mister,' said the big man, his voice spitting, 'you find that bitch you tell her from me she's dead! Do ya hear me? Goddamned dead!'

Well I started that pick-up and pulled out in a blanket of dust. Behind me in the mirror Lovely Winter was shaking his fist, then kicking at his cap on the ground. I looked forward, tried to focus my eyes on the road up ahead, but the thumping of my heart had gotten so bad now that I had to pull over, had to ease on that brake. I laid my head forward on my hands, felt as I did so something hard in my pocket. Sitting up, I pulled out the bottle, flipped off the cap. The pills were blue, the same shade as the bottle, each one decorated with the picture of some kind of bird. I held one to the light, felt the glow of its blue. I sat for a moment, turning it around. Then I put it on my tongue, took it back in my throat, closed my eyes and swallowed.

Now, from this distance, what I recall of the rest of that day – the road, the state line, that Arkansas hillside – is just a blur, a patchwork of faces rising up then passing by like the faces seen looming in some dream. And of course I cannot say that it was only the Doctor and his calming blue pills that made me say what I said and do what I did. No, sir. What happened that day – and all that has happened in these three months since – was, I believe, always destined to happen, though whether by God or fate I couldn't say. All I can say is – and of this I am certain – that when at last I found Audacity I didn't mean to hurt her, and all I can pray is that what she promised all those years ago she meant and that soon – any day now – she'll rid me of the past and I'll somehow find the strength to step out of my father's shadow.

11.00

From Nothing to Nowhere

Glenn Garon Songhurst was a musical rodeo rider who worked the Texas circuit back when the Texas circuit meant something. Previous to this he was in the Army; previous to that I don't know. If I was ever told, I can no longer remember. I believe he was born some-place in western Montana, but of this I can't be sure. Whatever, it was while he was in the Army that he met Dougie Fishbein and Gilber Creek, which is when I suppose his troubles really started. You see, when they got released, the three of them took to riding that circuit, each aiming to be the next Bo Dooley or Yakima Canutt – a target that turned out to be way out of reach for all but my daddy, and even he in the end wasn't close. Anyway, while Dougie went back to Arkansas and a life selling shoes door to door, and Gilber worked his way into becoming the Midwest's most respected painter of fake cattle-grids, my daddy stayed on. For five years, from the Gulf coast to the Oklahoma panhandle, from Texarkana in the east to El Paso in the south, he covered the same dusty roads again and again, staying in the same cheap motels or in the back of his old pick-up if he didn't make enough for a room, dreaming every year, every month, every day, that soon he'd break through to some kind of regular living, which of course he never did.

Anyway, as far as his act was concerned, people who saw it said it sure was a weird one. Billed as *Songs from the Saddle – a Novelty Act* (and himself as *The Minstrel of Moosic*), it involved, so I under-stand it, my daddy riding out to the center of the ring on the back of some arthritic old buffalo (yes, buffalo), from where, for a half-hour maybe, he'd perform.

Perform what? you say.

Well.

First, let me describe to you (to the best of my knowledge), a typical scene.

A rodeo arena – dust and blue skies, the smell of hot frying fat and sweat and old leather. There's good old boys squinting into the

44

sun, counting their day's winnings or lamenting their losings, then a feed-backing microphone announcing my daddy: Here he is, folks – Glenn Songhurst! Let's hear it for the man! Let's hear it for the Minstrel of Mooosic!' For a moment, then, there'd be silence, during which my daddy'd be trembling in the holding pen, his face a sort of white, his hands gripping his guitar and his knees locked tight around the shoulders of that animal. Though it was real ancient (and didn't trot so much as stagger), it was still an awful huge kind of creature that could crush a man's leg with one careless stamp or toss you, if it got up the mind to, high into the air like you were nothing but an old piece of rag, and you had to be real careful and treat it with some kind of respect or you'd probably live to regret it (or not, as the case may be). Anyhow, after maybe thirty seconds the pen door would rise and there he'd be – Glenn G. Songhurst, the Minstrel of Moosic – sitting high and smiling on the back of that buffalo as it sidled out to the center of the ring. Here, with the animal always looking around kind of stunned, my daddy would raise up his guitar and kick that beast into moving and they'd trot around the ring, the buffalo huffing and my daddy – despite the bouncing up and down that brought to his voice a kind of yodeling effect – singing and strumming songs of his own creation. Of these I'm told the most popular was a song called 'I Feel So Lonesome the Moment You're Gone It's Almost like Having You Here', which involved a passage of genuine yodeling, which, alongside the unintentional yodeling, made for something of a yodeling feast. This went on, as I've said, for maybe half an hour, although sometimes, if the response from the audience was good (good was pretty much anything above a silence), then he'd do a couple more songs, for which he'd get paid a few more dollars each, over and above his usual fee. In time, of course, even these few extra dollars didn't get to make up for his not having become a genuine rodeo rider, and he started to get careless, until, one day, he forgot to feed his buffalo and that buffalo just plain wouldn't move. Well there were whistles then from the crowd, and though in the end the show did go on (thanks only to six bucks' worth of edible bribes), Daddy knew that the end was coming.

He quit finally one freezing afternoon someplace near the Oklahoma line, when, having gassed up that old pick-up, he turned out his pockets only to discover that all he owned after five years of performing was twenty-three cents, half a pack of Lucky Strikes, a toll-booth token from the MacAnally Turnpike, and a pain in his gut from a hunger so bad that all he could hear was a pounding of the blood in his ears, and all he could see – though he believed that his eyes were deceiving him – was the figure of a young girl standing like a statue in the mist by the pumps.

Now, from this distance, whether it was fate or what that got my daddy to that gas station on that day I don't know, but whatever it was, it sure changed everything for him and my mama (not to mention me and Larry) – though on that day of course – the future being the closed thing it is – neither of them could possibly have known this. For both of them that day seemed like a day of endings not beginnings: for my daddy the hard waking from a dream of riding to riches, for my mama the ending of a one-month engagement to a young truck-driving man who'd chosen that very morning to scoot, leaving her with a six-year-old son (Larry), a whole heap of bitterness, an old guitar, and a boxful of clothes the very scent of which that morning – as she watched the stranger doubling up and crumpling to the ground – made her want to crumple too, made her want to start walking and to keep on walking, though she knew she had no place else to go.

So she just stood there watching, half listening for the growling sound of a returning truck that she knew in her heart was never going to come. For an hour then, two hours, she stood there on that bitter afternoon, freezing herself, until that thing that's inside of all of us – that thing that makes the living keep on living and the absence of which keeps the dead real still in their graves – rose up and took a hold of her, waking her. Even now, I can see her running her frozen hands through her hair that is as lank as string in the moist air. Turning, she catches her reflection in the window. She stares at herself staring back, amazed to find herself still standing.

It was a struggle of course – her being only slight and my daddy being the tall man he was – but somehow she managed to drag him over the forecourt and into the office. The office – empty that day as every day since her own daddy's passing thanks to the '54 measles epidemic – was lit by a single oil lamp and as quiet as a mortician's parlor. She leaned back against the desk, breathing hard. She tried not to think about anything.

From the office in a while she shifted the body into the back room where she heaved it – one end at a time – on to her mama's old settee. Here she left him. She closed the door behind her and went to check on Larry. Larry was sleeping and she watched him for a while. She closed her eyes, listening to the sounds of his breathing.

At six o'clock, when she'd stacked on the roadside all the things that the young truck-driving man had abandoned in his flight (all but the guitar, which, although she couldn't play, she reckoned she'd earned), she went back inside and lit the back-room fire. With the room warming, she gathered herself up in her daddy's old armchair and sat while the evening drifted on, watching.

Just what happened when at last the stranger came to depends on who you believe. To my daddy it was love at first sight; to my mama, though, it was different – something like pity – for, during the time she'd spent sitting in that chair watching him, breaking off now and then to jab at the fire with a stick, she'd come to the conclusion that she'd seen this man someplace before, and that whenever and wherever it was it had not been a happy occasion. But where, when? She couldn't think. It was only when, gone seven, he sat himself up and opened his eyes that it came to her.

She watched him rubbing his eyes with the palms of his hands.

'What happened?' he said.

'You fainted.'

'Fainted?'

In her mind's eye he was lying in the dirt at the Texarkana Rodeo, spitting stones through his teeth and cussing another hard fall.

'In the yard,' she said. In her memory there'd been tears of pain or something in his eyes, a buffalo stamping way off across the ring. He'd seemed to her then – sprawled at her feet looking up – like a little dusty boy who's just got beat in a schoolyard.

'Yard?' he said. 'What yard?' He tried to push up from the settee, but the pain in his head where he'd knocked it in his fall forced him back. He squinted through the low light. 'What you looking at?' he said.

'Nothing.'

'Well don't – okay?'

Mama shrugged. She could see the man was pale and probably starving. She thought of the soup she had simmering on the stove.

'Where am I?' he said.

Mama told him.

'What?'

'Nowhere,' she repeated.

'What do you mean, Nowhere?'

'Well you asked me where you are and I told you.'

Daddy closed his eyes tight, opened them. 'You mean this place is *called* Nowhere?'

Mama nodded.

'Oklahoma?' said Daddy.

'Uh-huh,' said Mama.

'Jesus Christ.'

'And Texas.'

'Pardon me?'

Mama touched her finger to the arm of her chair. 'This here's Oklahoma,' she said. She pointed then towards the settee. 'That's Texas.' Between them on the floor – between the floor and the settee – a white-painted line disappeared under a worn Cherokee rug, emerging the other side and heading to the wall.

'You mean – ' said Daddy.

'Uh-huh,' said Mama. It was then, she said, that something changed in the young man's eyes. For a moment the weariness and hunger slipped away, his eyes for a moment were brighter. He was staring at the white line, his look for a moment the look again of a child. He pushed himself up, a smile spreading over his face like an inverted shadow. 'Well, Jesus,' he said, and he stood then, placing one dusty boot in Texas and the other in this great state of Oklahoma.

Which – plainly told – is how my mama and daddy met – straddling two states. It is a moment – though unseen by me – that I shall always remember, and on days like today when I stand and look out across these vast empty lands, I know I shall always feel myself traveling back and back, ungrowing and unlearning, to that moment of my beginning long ago on that Oklahoma line.

11.50

The Camera Always Lies

I was speaking earlier of maybe going into town – to get the phone connected? Well I've been thinking some more about that, and the more I think about it the more certain I am that I should do it and as soon as possible. The longer I leave it the harder it's going to be, I know, and I know I'm going to have to go sometime – so why not now?

So then.

The trip.

Why haven't I gone already?

Well, I said also that I could maybe combine the phone business with the barn business – Bubba being in the frame so to speak for both things – and so I shall, which is the reason. I was all set to go (had my coat on and everything) when it occurred to me that it would be useful to take the barn's plans with me to show Bubba so he'll have some idea of the nature of the problem. Which of course means finding them first, which so far has proved difficult. It's for this reason then – my searching – that it's nearly noon already and I'm still here.

This and these papers.

Jesus, it's weird what you turn up. I haven't seen some of this stuff in years – some of it never. There's pictures and bills and all kinds of unidentifiable stuff – lists of things, even something that looks like an old bill of sale, maybe for Mama's gas station, I can't tell. There's everything it seems like but the plans of course. There's pictures of the barn – photos with me and Larry standing in front of it (I guess it must have been new and something to be proud of, though I don't remember) or Mama or Uncle Braxton (nose in the air as always, giving us that profile he always said was Roman, to which Daddy once said, 'Yeah, Rome, Indiana'), or Aunt Celeste and sometimes Dougie Fishbein or Gilber Creek; there's even one here someplace with Checker Noosefelt, back in the days when he still bought his belts off the rack at McGuire's and didn't have to

49

send all the way to Tulsa for belts so long (or so Larry and me used to think) you could wind them round the two of us twenty times and still have room for a sack of grain. In fact, there's pictures of that barn with pretty much everyone we knew standing in front of it (even Bubba and his brother Duane who took a bullet in the spine in Vietnam that let him linger on in Scranton for six weeks before he died) – everybody that is except Daddy himself who was always taking the pictures. The most you see of him ever is his shadow when the sun's behind him, broad at the legs and growing smaller as it peels its way over the yard or some fencepost, his arms crooked up in silhouette as he's holding the camera. Sometimes, the silhouette's so big it's almost as if it was that he was taking the picture of – as if he was checking it would actually come out, and that all that stuff Chief Yellowhammer used to say about how a man who's lost his soul will one day lose his shadow really was just the ramblings of some half-baked old mystic. Anyway, the point is that among all these pictures there's not one single picture of my daddy. I've searched and searched, but nothing. As the Hossman would say, 'It kinda makes you think' – although not in my case in a particularly healthy or constructive way. In fact the only thoughts I've been having sitting here have been entirely negative with regard to my daddy, which is something I must quit if the things I have to get done (like taking fresh flowers to Mama's grave) are going to get done.

So. Quit looking back and start looking forward is the thing to do right now, and I will. Just give me a minute and I'm gone. I just need a minute.

12.30

Night at the Fairview

Well I'm still here. Can I help it if things keep occurring to me –
patterns in things – that just will not go away? I cannot.

This time it's Doctor Rude again – him and his book *The Route
To Rude Health*, particularly that section on his father which, details
aside, could nearly have been written about mine. For the record, I
recall it went something like this:

> I never knew my father except through my mother's stories.
> She'd tell me how he'd always planned on being an astronaut,
> but that age and the end of the space program put an end to
> that. That he eventually wound up selling chili dogs at Wrigley
> Field was, she always said, often with tears in her eyes, an
> indictment of NASA's short-sightedness in particular, and of
> the American Way in general. 'Your father's life,' she told me
> more times than I could possibly recall, 'was a monumental
> tragedy of waste.' It was not, she said, the cancer that killed
> him, but the disappointment of a stunted life.

When I first read those words I could scarcely believe they were
the words of the man I had known at the Institute. Doctor Rude,
to me, had seemed for sure a man untainted by family tragedy, and
his attentions all the more precious for it. In a place where everyone's life was in some way a botched affair, his had seemed an
example of a life controlled (strange, perhaps, but controlled
nonetheless), and he a man untouched by the battering storms of
life. That this was far from the truth – that his life in reality was
nothing short of a monument to recovery and comeback – I only
learned through reading his book, and only then after leaving the
Institute. Had I known this before, I don't know how it might have
changed things. Maybe had I known he was really just one of us I
would not have listened so hard, not taken his word as such gospel.
Maybe, I don't know. All I do know is that *The Route To Rude Health*
really opened my eyes to the true greatness of the man – how he'd

fallen and risen so many times, and how he'd never lost his faith, his hope.

But back to that book.

I found it quite by chance, three days after my release, in a bargain bin at the Altus Wal-Mart on I-93. I'd gone in to pick up a change of clothes (I'd been wearing the same Institute clothes – a blue serge Rude Suit and socks the color of brick – for several weeks by now and I was starting to get some looks), and I was just on my way out when the face of a man I thought I knew caught my eye staring up at me from the corner of a book. For a second, gazing down at it sitting there drowning in a sea of other garish covers, I couldn't place it, but then suddenly those eyes and that thin face spoke to me, reminding me.

That I stole that book – that I just reached down, lifted it out, and walked as bold as you like through those hissing doors – I suppose you could say is proof itself of the Doctor's success. In times past, after all, fear of consequences would have stopped me acting, and had it not been for him and his methods, would, I guess, be stopping me acting to this day. *You worry too much, Mr Songhurst*: how many times have I heard him say that? A number beyond counting. Even today I can hear him saying it – see the way his pale lips would creep back from his teeth in that strange level smile of his – as clearly as I saw him that day maybe two weeks ago now gazing up at me from that bargain bin in Altus. That day, as I slipped behind the wheel of his old beat-up Pinto, I knew, really for the first time since I was a child, the careless serenity of living without worrying about tomorrow, and when I found myself looking at myself in the mirror and smiling, I felt sure that at last I had finally escaped the grip of the past.

That night, though, I wasn't so sure. That night, as I lay on my bed at the Fairview Motel, turning the pages of *The Route To Rude Health*, I was reminded again just how close the past always is to us and how we can never ever really escape, and the more I read that night of the Doctor's life – of his struggles with madness and the hollowness of a fatherless childhood – the more I was reminded of my own past life, and the more it seemed to creep in around me. Once again I thought of my own absent father, and of the hours and days I'd wasted as a child just longing for that telephone to ring, and the times I'd spent at this upstairs window, searching the horizon for the dust from his wheels that never once appeared.

I slept that night, but fitfully. My dreams when they came came hard and sharp – bitter vignettes whose bitterness woke me and set me to staring bleary-eyed at the darkness and listening to the hissing of cars on the highway and the sharp-edged fragments of voices in my head. *So long,* said my daddy, hands gripping tight to the wheel of his car, his breath rising warm through the cold spring air. *So long – you take care of your mama, y'hear?* And then he was gone and it was just me and Mama and Larry of course, and we stood there the three of us unwilling to turn away, although soon there was nothing more to see but the distant trees swaying against the sky, and nothing to hear but Uncle Braxton chopping wood in the yard.

That day – so many years ago now – I recall as clearly as if it were yesterday. Even today, as I sit here surrounded by these pictures, looking out at those same trees now grown, I can still place to the inch where I stood on that road, and still – when I listen – hear the whooshing of Uncle Braxton's ax and the splitting of that wood, and the beating in my ears of my own infant heart.

1.00

In the Beginning Was the Turd

The moment I first laid eyes on Ike Rude I knew for sure he was madder even than me. He was squatting on the desk in his office with his pants around his ankles, having just delivered himself of a turd so immense and of such smooth contours that I was certain it was fake – one of those joke-store turds you leave on the school bus to frighten all the girls and piss off the driver.

Which is exactly of course what it was.

'You see this?' he said, still squatting, lifting the thing between finger and thumb. 'You know what this is?'

'It's a turd,' I said, never having been one not to state the obvious.

'Indeed,' said the Doctor. 'The crap of the human heart.' He spun, half rolled off the desk and pulled up his pants. He leaned back as if suddenly short-sighted. 'From this,' he said, squinting at the item in question and turning it around gravely, 'were it genuine, I could tell you the name of my grandaddy's grandaddy, or the number of times I've had soup on a Tuesday.' He looked up. 'What do you think of that, Mr Songhurst?'

I shrugged. Lately there'd been so many weird things happening to me that one more barely signified. 'I guess that's real useful,' I said.

At this, as if I'd said something wholly significant, Doctor Rude raised his eyebrows in an arch. It was a gesture I would come to know well. 'Hmmm,' he said. He stood up. Then, without taking his eyes off me, as if he thought I might bolt any second (if only he'd known I barely had the energy to breathe), he moved away from the desk with that gliding walk of his that made you think he'd suddenly acquired a pair of roller skates and across to the shelves behind me. I heard him rustling some papers. I let my eyes close. I was just drifting off into the arms of sleep when a voice said sharply, 'You ever see a stool pigeon, Mr Songhurst?'

I opened my eyes.

'Mr Songhurst?'

I turned. 'What?' I said. My eyes were smarting from lack of sleep.

'A pigeon,' said the Doctor, a trace of impatience creeping into his voice, 'of the stool variety.' He was holding a sheet of paper by his side. This he lifted and held against his chest. On it was a crude child-like drawing of some kind of bird. The bird – oval like a football with long skinny legs and no discernible head – was standing over what looked to be a pile of rocks.

'Well?' said the Doctor.

I shook my head. No sleep for three days and three nights had finally taken its toll. I could hardly keep my eyes open.

The Doctor glanced at the drawing. He smiled indulgently as if at a wayward but favorite child, then looked up again. 'Well I didn't really think so. Such a bird, you see, Mr Songhurst, is rare. Rarer, indeed, than the one-legged icebird.'

'Icebird?' I said.

'Icebird, Mr Songhurst. A nocturnal bird found exclusively on the floes of Saskatchewan. A creature so in tune with the ebb and flow of nature that it scares us, Mr Songhurst, and what scares us of course we murder – do we not?' He arched his brows, inviting a response. Of course I turned away. My head was spinning. The man, quite clearly, was even crazier than I'd first thought. I pushed myself up. 'Look – ' I said.

'Leaving us?' said the Doctor. 'Checking out are we?'

I turned to face him. The drawing was now on the table beside him, his arms folded in a gesture of challenge. He smiled. 'Well that's okay. We don't have prisoners here. You can of course check out any time you like. Just walk the walk, Mr Songhurst, and you're out of here. As free, you might say, as a bird.'

'Okay,' I said, 'I will.' And I took a step forward to the door, then another. As I twisted the handle and pulled I could feel eyes boring into the back of my head.

The corridor was broad, the floors highly polished. Perhaps two dozen doors opened off from either side. On this day all the doors were closed, their wire-mesh windows blinded. I walked on down the corridor, aware with every step of the squeak of my soles on the hard waxy floor. I pushed on the doors at the end, expecting some resistance. None came. I drew a breath and stepped outside. The air was winter sharp, the ground frozen hard. Breathing in hurt my lungs; breathing out made a shaft like smoke, the width of a man's arm. It spun out horizontal to the earth then broke and billowed, losing itself against the bleached October sky. I stood for a moment staring up, trying to think how I'd got there, my eyes following the arc of a high-flying plane. I tried to imagine the passengers inside the plane and some far-off exotic destination but could not, and in the end I gave up trying. I crossed the empty basketball court, heading for the white fields and the Interstate beyond. With every step I expected something – a hand on my arm, the crack of a rifle maybe – but of course nothing came. I searched the uneven ground ahead of me as I walked, all the way up to the highway and beyond. No fences. Nothing. Nothing between me and the rest of the world.

I'd been walking for maybe ten minutes when something made me stop and look back. The buildings of the Institute were far off now, hunkered down as if gathered for warmth against the earth, the windows blind white, reflecting the sky. It looked deserted like a mall on Christmas Day, the parking lot around the side empty of all cars but one. This – some kind of small car, dirty white like the ground – sat alone in the corner of the lot, the words on its side – OKLAHOMA INSTITUTE OF RUDE HEALTH – scuffed and barely visible in the grime. I remember now how it seemed so out of place to me – an incongruous connection to the world outside. As I stood there blinking in the cold air, I tried to imagine its wheels turning or its indicators flashing, signaling some intention, but could not. It seemed to me as rooted in that hard ground as the buildings themselves and the skeleton trees that shivered now and then in the chill moist air. I pulled up the collar of my coat and turned away. My feet and hands were freezing. As I started walking, hobbling on the numbness in my boots, I felt on my face the first snow of the season as it wandered idly down.

Looking back now, I can no longer recall where it was I thought I was going on that day. Maybe I didn't know. What I do recall is slipping and sliding my way up a shallow bank, grazing the palms of my hands and my knees, then standing in the weeds on the edge of the Interstate, watching my breath pouring out like steam and waiting for something – anything – to come down that empty road.

And waiting, and waiting.

But of course nothing came. Nothing and nobody was out on that bitter day. I squinted at the emptiness through the now thick-falling snow, but all was quiet, unmoving. I started walking – thinking of the plane I'd seen before and searching the sky for it – and I was walking still and stumbling now and then in the scrub when the sky grew suddenly dark and the landscape rose up around my shoulders and I found myself lost in some trees.

I stopped, looked around me. The trees were thick, a tangle of uprights arching over me and blocking the light, the ground at my feet so moist now that I felt as if I were sinking. I heard a rustling far off; I turned. There were shapes in the darkness, shifting, the echo of something in the earth. I turned again and started walking, but the harder I walked the more the earth seemed to hinder me, rising up root-shaped and clawing at my ankles until at last I knew I would fall.

When I hit the ground I hit it hard – hard enough as it turned out to dislocate my jaw. I tried to sit up, but the pain told me no. I closed my eyes. This it it, I thought, at last, and I let go my limbs.

Minutes pass then in my memory, slow like hours. When at last I opened my eyes I was lying on my back in a cool green room, a face – a woman's – looming over me and smiling.

I squinted, tried hard to focus. I eased my hand out from under the covers and touched my face. My jaw was wired, my lips cracked and dry.

'You had a bad fall,' said the woman – Experience Boothe from her name badge – and she leaned forward over me, fixing something behind my head, bringing to me as she did so a familiar smothering scent. 'In Miller's Copse. You were lucky the Doctor found you. You could have froze on a night like that.' She straightened up, frowning. 'What's that?' she said. She studied my lips as I tried hard to speak. 'How long?'

I nodded.

'Two days,' she said softly.

Two days?

'Which reminds me.' She reached down out of my sight to something on a chair. 'This is for you.' She lifted my right hand, wrapped my fingers around a package. The package was thin and square, brightly wrapped and tied with a bow. 'From the Doctor.'

Two days? Two whole days?

Experience Boothe frowned at my confusion, then brightened. 'For your birthday,' she explained, then she turned and in a moment was gone.

Slowly, with aching fingers, I opened the package, letting the wrapping fall. Before me, framed, set behind polished glass, was the football-shaped bird with its long spindly legs. *For Billy Songhurst*, read the caption, *From One Lark to Another.*

That was nearly three months ago now. Since then so much has happened, the time truly flown just as the Doctor predicted it would. 'It'll soon be Christmas and you'll be home,' he told me many times, and now, in two days, it will be so. In two days, along with the rest of the ghosts in this house (and with those, I suppose, in the rest of America, not to mention the rest of the world) I will celebrate, here, the birth of Our Savior, give thanks for His coming for to take away my sins.

1.42

Eyes of the Buffalo

I believe I have come recently to be something of an expert on the many different ways there are of cooking eggs – which is just as well as, aside from a few cans of peaches in syrup, eggs is just about all there is. There were some old potato chips and a half-dozen cans of artichoke hearts left over from God knows when, but that's all gone now, which leaves me as I said with just these eggs. Eggs boiled, eggs scrambled, eggs poached, eggs fried, eggs sunnyside up or over easy: you name it, over these last few days I've cooked it. Two days ago I even tried an omelet, though this was not too successful and I have not repeated the exercise since. In fact I would not repeat any of them probably ever again if I didn't have to, I'm getting that sick of them. What I'd give right now for some nice piece of steak I could not begin to tell you.

But, hey. You're right. These eggs and the various ways of cooking them are not what I was planning to mention here. What it was was the trip and these thoughts I've been having with regard to Bubba. It was thinking about God and sin that did it, and wondering if Bubba knows what I've done. If he does, then it kind of changes things, and it's this – thinking about him knowing, thinking about that look of disgust in his eye – that has frozen my limbs like this so that I'm wondering right now if I've even got the strength to make it up to Mama's grave, let alone into town. In fact right now I'm wondering if I'll ever move again, or if maybe, when they find me, they'll find me frozen, standing up, my hands clutching these eggs and my eyes looking blind like the eyes of some buffalo whose eyes have seen mine and whose ears have heard this silence in my heart.

2.16

The Dead Are Not to Blame

So at last it's done and I should be glad I know – and I would be if it weren't for the fact that it occurred to me on my way back from Salter's Field how unfortunate it was that I should have mentioned Alice last night in such a negative light. It was wrong of me I see now to imply that she was in any way responsible for the terrible thing I did, or that she should feel (wherever she is) guilty for an absence which has recently come to trouble me greatly. The dead are not – and should never be – to blame for the troubles attending the living; to blame them so is evidence of a weak and shallow nature. So, that said, all I should further say on the matter is that I apologize, and to promise, during my waking hours at least, not to repeat the offense. I would promise for the night-time too, but such a promise would not be worth even the breath with which it is uttered. Like every other living soul I have no control over dreams: if I call out I call out. There's nothing I can do about it except wait to wake, and even then sometimes when I do they're all still there – Mama and Daddy and Larry and –

But no. For security's sake I will not even think of her. I will force myself to think of other things – snow, for example, the continued absence of which (despite Sonia the Weathergirl's smiling assurances that it really is coming) has recently been exercising my mind – so much so lately that I've developed this theory. Lately, I've come to the conclusion that just about nothing of any significance in my life has ever happened without the ground being covered with the stuff. For example, the snow was on the ground on the day I met Audacity and on the day three years later, three months ago now (can it really only be three months?) when I watched her drive away. It was falling, too, later, when I did what I did in that Arkansas field, and again when I stood at the doors of the Institute. That was the last time. Since then, since my arrival here at the farm, there's been nothing but threats. *Any day now,* Sonia says every night, but every day it's just the same – cold enough, God knows, but just the same. Nothing. For which I suppose I should be grateful, and one half of me is. One half of me's glad for the barn's sake, while the other half can't stop searching the skies. This half of me just can't help believing that only a snowfall will really bring Audacity, and that waiting without one is useless. Crazy I know – but what can I do? And how can I win when one half of me is destined to lose?

3.17

First Memory

A tiny figure in the desert, dark against the snow-bound land: this, then, my first memory of Audacity. She is searching for something, down on her hands and knees, when suddenly she hears my car, looks up. I touch the brakes, grind on to the shoulder; she stands, waves her hands, frantic. I pull up alongside, buzz the window. You okay? I say. Didn't you see me? she says. See you? I say. Waving, she says. She is squinting, her hair – copper now – flaring in the light. Contacts, she says, I dropped them, and now – She shakes her head, looks down at my wheels. How could I be so dumb?

This, then, first meeting.

And the last?

Amarillo of course, Louie's death and the shouting, then her driving away, and then –

But no. Everything in its place. Order is everything.

So. That day.

The day after Mama's funeral.

I was driving west out of state and into Texas, just trying not to think about anything, just trying to drive and not think about Mama or Larry's doing time (again) way up in Kentucky, and certainly not my failure (again) with Louie in the barn – just trying to think about the road ahead and the gig that night at the festival in Demming. For reasons that I'll get to, Demming wasn't a place I wanted to play at all, but now am I glad that I did. After all, had I not been driving down that highway heading west then chances are I'd never have met Audacity. Of course she wasn't Audacity then at all – just plain (in the name sense) Audrey McGuane, daughter – one of three – of Mr Stewland McGuane, a former chief fire officer on a rig down in the Gulf.

Anyhow, that day.

She learned forward, folded her arms on my door, 'Well?' she said.

'Well what?' I said. Her face was the most regular face I'd ever seen – one side duplicated exactly in the other.

'I asked you how come you're so dumb.'

I shrugged. Her skin was clear tan, her eyes ocean green.

'You don't know?' She huffed. Her collarbones lifted like tiny oars, fell back. 'Maybe it just comes natural, huh?'

'Maybe it does,' I said. I gripped the wheel. 'So you want a ride or not?'

She frowned. 'What about my contacts?'

'I'm not asking you to steer.'

She turned away for a moment, looking back down the road. I glanced at her shoulder, at the pulse in her neck. My own heart was thumping so loud I felt sure she'd hear it. I touched the gas; the engine growled. 'Of course,' I said, 'if you'd rather stay here – '

She turned back, cocked her head to one side in that way she had of considering things. 'How do I know you ain't no pervert? How do I know you ain't gonna jump on me as soon as I get in your car?'

'Well I guess you don't,' I said.

She frowned again, but in back someplace lurked a smile.

'Besides,' I said, 'how do I know *you're* not gonna jump *me*?'

The smile crept closer. 'Why,' she said, 'would anyone wanna be jumping you?'

'It has been known.'

She shook her head, as if dismissing the notion as absurd. 'Well, thanks to you crushing my lenses I can't see to do no jumping, can I? So I guess you'd be safe.'

'In that case I guess you're safe too.'

'Oh yeah?'

'I've given up jumping blind women. These days it's only women that can see they're being jumped that take my attention. I've found them to be more of a challenge.'

Suddenly that smile bloomed fresh across her face.

'Well?' I said, I was smiling too, I couldn't help it.

'Okay,' she said. She circled the car and got in.

That day, all day, we drove clean across Texas. Slid down in the front seat, her sneakers on the dash, Audacity told me as we drove what amounted to the story (so far) of her life. She was, she said, an only child born to parents to whom a child was a gift from God. Her mother, she said, was the Angel of Angels, her father a carpenter with smooth hands that were never raised in anger. Living still, she said, in a house on the Texas shore, they read books and newspapers (not just the funnies), and on Thanksgiving Day they'd run up a flag. There was a room in their house, she said, always waiting for her – a house and a room from which, she said, she had only recently come. Where was she going? To a cousin, she said, who ran a clothes store in Encino, California, where, she said, she would stay for a month, maybe two. Encino, she'd heard, was the place to go; Encino had the climate, the ocean, everything. It was a story so rich in American ghosts, and so obviously nothing but lies. I glanced at her now and then, laughing when she laughed: she never once returned my look. Her eyes she kept fixed on the distant horizon as if it was the future and only the future that mattered or even existed.

It was falling dusk when we crossed into New Mexico. The day was cooling fast, the winter sun dipping down behind the mesas in the west. I flicked on the lights. 'You okay?' I said. She'd been quiet for a while. I glanced over. 'Audrey?' Her eyes were closed. I turned on the radio low. I pulled up the collar of my coat. *George Strait*, growled the Hossman, *Easy Come, Easy Go*. I stretched my arms, settled back, drove on.

Audrey McGuane was sleeping still when I pulled off the highway at the Santa Rosa exit and into the parking lot at General Thrifty's Economotel. I cut the engine; she stirred, lifted her weary head. 'Where are we?' she said. She looked around, squinting, bleary-eyed like a child. 'Why've we stopped?'

'It's after midnight,' I said.

'So?'

'So I needed a rest.'

She shrugged. 'Oh, okay. Sure.' She straightened up, drew the handles of her bag across her shoulder. 'Well thanks, okay?' She pulled on the door's handle. The door swung open, filling the cab with the night's cold air.

'What're you doing?' I said.

She was halfway out of the cab. She turned, squinting, scowling. 'What?'

65

'Well it's dark for one thing,' I said.

'So?'

'So you can't just go – '

'Can't I? Who says I can't?'

'Well – '

She pushed out, slammed the door, started walking away. For a moment I just watched her, her lightness, the careful way she slipped between the silent cars, and I'd probably have sat there all night, just watching, had something from way down inside of me not stung me and forced me out of that truck, not filled my lungs with that cold air, not made me call out her name.

She stopped, her back to me. I heard myself calling again.

'So what is it?' she said, far off, her breath rising.

'Where're you going?' I said.

She turned in a pool of yellow light. 'I told you,' she said. 'Encino. You have a problem with that?'

I shrugged, looked over to the highway. It was clear – no cars. 'I just thought you wanted a ride is all.'

'I'll get a ride.'

'It sure don't look too likely.' The road was clear way into the night – no lights, no sounds of oncoming cars, no blasts from truckers' horns. 'Still,' I said, 'if that's what you want – ' I turned away; my heart was beating fast. I walked back to the pick-up, started unroping the cover. In a while there were footsteps behind me.

'So?'

'So what?' I said. The rope was wet from the snow and tough to pull out of the hooks.

'So what's the idea?'

'What?'

'Calling me like that.'

'No idea,' I said. Behind me I heard a boot grinding dirt.

'Billy?'

'That's my name.'

'Look – ' She paused, more grinding. 'Look – if I stayed – and I ain't saying I am, right? – I wouldn't want nothing to happen, right?'

I yanked off the last of the ropes.

'Look,' I said, turning, 'if you stay – and I ain't saying I'm gonna let you, right? – I can promise you nothing's gonna happen.'

She frowned, cocked her head. 'Are you telling me you're gay or something?'

'No, Audrey,' I said. 'I'm not telling you I'm gay. I'm not telling you I'm anything.'

'So what are you telling me?'

'What I'm telling you is that, with the kind of chaperone we've got, then for sure nothing's gonna happen – not even, Audrey, if you promised me a gig at the Grand Ole Opry.'

Audrey McGuane set her hands on her hips. I could see in her eyes that she thought I was mad.

'Chaperone?' she said. 'What chaperone?'

I pulled back the pick-up's canvas cover. 'Meet Louie,' I said, whereupon Louie B. Songhurst, long-ago nemesis of long-gone Uncle Braxton, not to mention the heaviest goose ever recorded west of the Mississippi river, raised his head, cocked an eye, and let rip a blast of wind that I reckon could be heard all the way across the state and halfway to the stars in the sky.

'He did what?'

Later that night, when I'd told her my story – about Daddy and Larry and those years on the farm, and how the farm was empty with Mama gone too now, how these rooms – once so filled up with noise, with life – were silent now, I told her about Louie and how, years ago, he'd killed Uncle Braxton and how – just hours passed – I'd failed with the shotgun in the barn.

'You mean for real?' she said.

'For real,' I said.

We were sitting – the three of us – in the Antietam Suite, Louie blinking in the light, his head clicking left, right, left, right, as he watched a game of tennis on cable. With every changeover, every set of commercials, he'd turn towards us, cocking his head as if he was listening.

'But I just couldn't do it,' I said. 'I was standing there all ready to shoot, but I just couldn't.' I glanced at Louie; despite a tie-break on the TV he was staring right at me.

'Well, of course you couldn't do it,' said Audrey. She turned,

67

smiling, to Louie. 'How could anyone ever think of doing such a thing?' Louie clicked his head a turn to consider her. When she stood up and approached him he took to gargling that special warning way down in his throat.

'Audrey,' I said, 'I wouldn't do that if I were you – '

'Do what?' She reached out a hand.

'Audrey – '

Oh Jesus. 'Audrey!' I braced myself for the loss of fingers, for the screams of distress in the night. None came. In their place, from Louie came a strange kind of cooing and a look of rich pleasure in his eye.

'There now,' said Audacity, her fingers caressing his temples, 'ain't you a handsome boy, huh?' Her eyes flicked to mine, burned a moment, flicked away. She kissed Louie's head. 'Hey now, Louie,' she said, 'ain't you just a girl's special friend?'

That night, with Louie sleeping exhausted on the floor, Audacity and I clung together in the darkness. I breathed as she breathed, felt the sanctuary of her limbs around mine as she slept. When she woke at four and said, 'Billy?' I held her tighter still, felt the rhythm of her crying in my chest. 'I know,' I whispered when she told me she'd lied – that there was no house on the Texas shore, no cousin in Encino, no Angel of Angels, no carpenter's smooth hands never raised in anger – then we drifted together, breathing together, headed in time toward dream-filled sleep. I dreamed, first, that when I woke it had all been just a dream; then I dreamed that I was back on the farm again, that Mama and Daddy were together again, that everything for so long so lost had been found once again complete and brand-new, sparkling like the sun in some clear morning sky.

4.57

Never Walk Alone

I have temporarily abandoned my search for those plans. I know this means also – for the moment at least – shelving the trip into town, but so be it. There's no point going without them, and besides it's not as if the barn (or the phone) is the only problem around here that needs addressing. There's also Christmas – in particular the matter of the little baby Jesus, and how, here, given my present circumstances, I might best celebrate his birth. Simple you might say: decorate a tree and sing a bunch of carols and bingo it's a done deal. Well let me tell you, simple it may sound but simple it is not. For one thing I have no tree (nor, for that matter, could I lay my hands on any decorations without starting another search like my first – and so far failed – one), and for another I couldn't sing those carols without breaking my current ban on singing. So – what else is there? Aside from the food which I also don't have (it's that trip into town again for that), not a whole lot. Gifts of course are out of the question (both giving and receiving), as is any kind of party or family get-together. Apart from Audacity (and God knows where she'll be; today I'm seriously doubting it'll be here), there's only really Larry anyway, and he's, well, where he is. I guess all in all you could say this whole coming season seems a little bleak; in fact it would be entirely so if it weren't for one unexpected thing.

If I said it's a kind of peace I'm feeling right now, a sort of pleasant kind of numbness, it might sound a little strange, which maybe it is. Whatever, right now peaceful is how I'm feeling (despite all my problems and shortcomings) and the reason for it is as follows. It is that, right now, I am certain that God has forgiven me for what I've done. Just how I know this I couldn't say – I just know it. He has looked down upon me and lifted the burden of my guilt and given me, by so doing, a second chance at things. *Billy,* He has said, *get up off your knees and don't look back, look forward, embrace the future as for so long you've embraced the past. Walk on and on with hope in your heart, for you'll never walk alone –*

But there I go. Singing when I just said I wouldn't. Ah, what the hell. How did a little singing ever hurt anybody? You'll be saying next that drinking's out too. Jesus Christ. Soon there'll be nothing to do here that's worth doing. Soon there'll be nothing to do but breathe. Soon I'll have nothing but air.

6.00

Leaving Space

Three weeks after their meeting at the gas station, Mama and Daddy were married in a snowstorm at the church of St Stephen's in the small west Oklahoma town of Space. By all accounts the ceremony was lucky to have happened at all, old Reverend Winters (truly his name) having fallen the night before on the church's icy steps and having spent the entire night where he fell. Indeed, if it hadn't been for Clara Willets happening by around six (thanks to her having had words with her own fiancé Duane and then storming out, thus postponing her own forthcoming marriage), people said he would probably have froze to death. As it was, being rescued when he was, he wasn't so far gone that he couldn't thaw out, and come the following morning he was there at the altar, the only sign of his mishap being the arm he held heavy in a sling and a look on his face midway between fright and thankfulness that, according to Mama, he never did lose. 'Till the day I die,' she used to say, 'I shall never forget the worries we had, your daddy and me, over whether he was gonna make it through, what with his shaking and his keeping on losing the ring in his cast – ' Well he did make it through of course, and the vision I have of him when the ceremony was through – some frail old man waving through a blizzard from the steps of his church at the couple he's just joined together in the sight of God disappearing through the thick-falling snow – is a vision I shall never forget. It's right up there with other scenes I never really witnessed except through others' eyes – my daddy, for example, hanging on to the saddle on the back of some wild kicking beast like his life depended on it (which it pretty much did) or the hurt of the failure in his eye on the day he arrived with his new bride – needing charity – on this his brother's farm, or my mama on those days before the wedding standing still at that gas station window wondering if my daddy was just something from a dream and whether, if he was real, he'd still be there when the spring came and the summer. Even today – especially today – these and

71

other secondhand memories crawl over me at night and into my dreams, and I watch them playing over and over until, at times like these, I feel drugged on the power of the past and I find myself dozing like an old man on Sunday, unable to move beneath its suffocating weight, snow-blind to the future that in my brightest moments I know must surely come.

Thursday

4.00

Stillness and Shadows

Dawn rises, morning's here at last. At last the light bleeds in, folding over the arm of this chair. See how the colors bloom, see how memory falters. Can it really be me sitting here? These arms, these hands – can they really be my arms, my hands? See how they turn, these hands, fingers stretching in the light, feel the dust spinning, watch it settle.

Stillness.

Shadows.

Hear how the morning creeps. Listen. A bird, way off; a heart close at hand. A hand turns, cuts the air, settles over a heart. Feel it, how it beats, my heart, how it pumps, hear the blood thumping heavy in my ears.

Another day of life, one more off the calendar.

Sssh.

Look. Watch the darkness receding, drawing over the land. Hear it dragging its heavy boots.

5.21

The Spectaculo Dancing School

I've just paced this room and found it to be approximately fifty foot by seventy – not including the fireplace alcove. Along one wall there's a mirror perhaps fifteen foot wide and five foot deep that was a leaving gift to Aunt Celeste from the Spectaculo Dancing School for whom, until her marriage to Uncle Braxton the year after his leaving the Army, she performed the dual roles of pianist and chili cook, chili being the only food that the school's patron, Mrs Evangeline Eliot, would allow to be served on the premises. On the opposite wall there is, as you can see, a series of windows from which, on a clear day, you can just about make out the steeple on top of the First Church of God, along with the Glories I mentioned yesterday. To be honest, how they got this name I have no idea (if you've seen one silo then truly you have seen them all) – all I know is that that's what people call them and have always called them and I suppose always will. Anyway, aside from these windows and that mirror, there's the piano, three chairs, this settee, a bureau, the TV in its fake wood cabinet, three tattered rugs, a collection of framed pictures so faded now I can barely make them out, and a bookcase with glass doors from which the contents have long since been removed and – I imagine – sold. I suppose all in all, what with the age and general disrepair of everything (everything but the TV which never seems to decay), the whole feel of the room is one of gloom – enough sometimes to get a man so depressed that he can get to wishing he was someplace else or even, sometimes, no place at all. Sometimes it can all feel so heavy with what's been that you just want to rest back and close your eyes, just let it all come around, just let it hold you like the arms of a lover and never in this lifetime let you go.

Though not, as I say, this morning. This morning, first thing, I was struck with the sudden strong need to kill off this killing silence, if only for a while, if only to remind myself what the sounds of life are like.

Hence the piano, and me, here, these keys.
Hence this song, going something like this.

7.15

Other Voices, Other Hands

Sometimes I can't believe what's happening. Sometimes it's like it was all just somebody else and someplace else, and like all I know of it is all I've seen on some show on TV, and that flicking that dial I can just turn it off, turn away. But I can't. I close my eyes and it's always there and when I open them too. Day or night makes no difference. What's done is done and can never be undone. There's always something there, reminding me. Always something sitting there and blocking my way.

Like this piano, for instance, this morning. I sing and it's not just me singing, play and it's not just me playing. There's always other voices, other hands. Some from way back – so far back sometimes I can hardly hear them though they're always there, whispering, words coming to me like whispers through a wall, the faint kiss of breathing on my neck. I twist and turn; they twist and turn too. They are dogged, these voices, and mornings these days they will not let me go. This morning they followed me, swirled around me as I sat, brought to me as I sang their voices from the past. There was Aunt Celeste and me and Miss Dean at the dancing school, the smell of sweat and polished wood, the air hanging still on a Friday three o'clock, and voices clipping sharp in the schoolyard next door. The door closes, Aunt Celeste's footsteps grow faint in the hall and I am back there, a child again, fingers sticky on these keys. I play, the sound echoes, Bach, clumsy, all thumbs, then Miss Dean's there – here – beside me, her scent in my nostrils and her hands on my hands as we play the Spectaculo Dancing School Song, playing on until the last note is done and it's kisses goodbye and I'm running down the street through sunshine.

Truly it seems there are some things you can never forget: the cawing of rooks in misty trees; Elvis on Ed Sullivan, waist up; Fridays, for me, those hands on my hands and the feel of these keys, then the touch of those lips on my cheeks. *Play it again Billy – shall we?* And we do, over and over, until the shadows grow longer and creep over our limbs, and it's time to run home for supper. You know I can still see those charms on Miss Dean's bracelet – the tiny silver boot, the gentleman's top hat – feel the smoothness still of her fingers, their gentle pressure on my chin. A little kiss for Miss Dean, then it's run down Main Street, turn right at the hydrant outside Billow Fashions, cross the street without looking (were there ever any cars?) and only slow down when the town's slipping back and all I can see is the fields and the dust and to my left way off the Glories turning crimson with the light, while to my right there's Uncle Braxton and Raymond of course – two tiny figures – fixing fenceposts with a mallet, the sound hanging muffled in the cold air. I stand again in the trees, watching Raymond in that thick winter coat that he wore through every season raising the mallet then letting it fall, then, turning away, I see Daddy again, just a ghost on the highway, his ghost car growing smaller, heading south to the circuit, the rasp of his muffler growing faint until it's gone.

And then? Then nothing. Just the silence of absence, just this distant piano, just this landscape of days stretching on.

Chief Yellowhammer Welcomes You

Oh Lord, I must rise up, pull myself out of this morning sloth. It's gone ten already and I'm still sitting here, still unwashed, still unbreakfasted. For sure if anything's going to get done today then I really must get going. God knows there's enough I have to do.

That trip for one thing.

And those plans. Frankly they could be anywhere. And what if they no longer exist? What if they never existed at all? What if my memory of them is just something come from dreams? And even if they do exist someplace and I do find them – what then? For all I know Bubba could be dead by now or way across the country, or the plans just useless, or maybe the barn's so bad it's beyond repair. And even if Bubba is there and the barn does get repaired – so what? What exactly will I have achieved? It's just a barn after all – it's not like it's some kind of shrine that must be preserved for future generations. It's just a rickety old barn – nothing more – and I'm thinking right now it might just be best to let the thing tumble and be done with it, and maybe if it does carry anything with it – spirits of the past or whatever – well, so be it. Maybe it's best to just let things go, let the past be the past and get buried.

But I can't do it. I wish I could but I can't. It's always there – here – sitting there watching me as I'm watching it. Even now. Even now as I sit here willing myself to rise and get going, I am dreaming the past just as it was. Even now, sitting here on Aunt Celeste's old settee, I can feel the snow on my daddy's face and the tears in my mama's eyes as the gas station slips away behind them, feel the ring on her finger and the chill of her future in her blood. I turn now as she turns, gaze at the man she has contracted to love. 'Darlin'?' he says; she nods, draws up a smile. The car rumbles on. *Love is only needing made in blood*: this she heard once in a song and it returns to her now, and her heart flutters as she thinks of the long-ago father of her son, of the glare of his teeth, white by the light on the night-stand. She wonders where he is now and what he's doing, then she tells herself he's probably dead, killed on some back road by the drinking that was always going to kill him, then she thinks of the young truck-driving man and she folds her hands. She turns, looks out, sees herself looking back, her face as white as a ghost's. His face, she recalls, was as brown as burnt wheat, his fingers lean as a girl's as he picked that guitar or played rhythm on her back and neck. She closes her eyes, feels again the creep of his fingers. *I love you because*, he says, mimicking a voice on the radio. Why? she says, fishing. *Because you understand, dear*, he sings and he laughs then and covers her with his shadow. She can smell him, taste the salt of his skin, is feeling again the warmth of him when the car hits a bump and jolts her awake. 'Darlin'?' says her husband, 'are you feelin' hungry?' She nods, feels the car turning, hears Larry on the back seat stirring, feels the miles already traveled and the miles yet to come spinning away behind her and she grips the seat to stop herself falling but she can't stop herself falling and the sickness that's been visiting her for weeks now rises up in her like panic and the seat's hot and there's cold creeping over her like fingers and she has to get out but she can't get out and then everything's glary then black then nothing and she's slipping, floating down and away –

'Darlin'?' says the voice again. She answers but hears nothing. Something slams – a door – then footsteps on gravel. I'm dying inside, she thinks calmly, and the last thing she sees is a row of little Cherokee dolls smiling at her as she passes by, as, spreading her fingers and arching her back, she passes away into sunlight.

Next thing, she's lying on a bench, she feels the plastic beneath her. Opening her eyes she sees lights, glaring, then a face.

'Madam?' The stranger's jaw is working, the face a deep brown. Dark hair surrounds the face, gathered, beaded. Breath sweet as berries tumbles over her. She tries to sit up but cannot. Her eyes close. She is floating. I am dreaming, she thinks, then she is.

When she wakes the dark face is gone, in its place another.

'Darlin'?'

She opens her mouth to speak. Her mouth is dry. A hand touches hers.

'Darlin'? Are you feelin' okay?'

'Glenn?' she says, the word just a whisper.

He smiles.

'Where's Larry?'

'He's okay. Sleeping.'

She squints in the light. 'What happened?'

'You fainted.'

'Fainted?'

Again he smiles. 'Your turn.'

She frowns, but then she remembers – the gas-station forecourt, the crumpling stranger. She remembers also the wedding in the snow, the preacher with his arm in a sling.

'Darlin' – can you sit up?'

Again she tries, this time pushing through the pounding. The face of the truck-driving man comes close to her, smiling; she pushes it away.

'Glenn?'

The face withdraws, is replaced by another – the dark face, Cherokee or Chickasaw.

'Madam?'

'Who are you?' she says. She feels a hand on her belly. She tries to push away. 'What – '

The Indian is smiling, his hand firm and cool.

'Madam,' he says, soothing. 'Be calm. You are safe.' His hand is warm now, encasing hers. His teeth, she sees, are white as stripped bone.

'Where am I?' she says, then her eye catches words printed bright on a button: CHIEF YELLOWHAMMER'S MOTEL – SAY POW! SAY WOW!

She frowns again, looks again at the face. Something moves behind him. She focuses. The other man – her husband, she sees now – is examining the elbow of his jacket. 'Glenn?' she says. He looks up.

'Darlin'?' He steps forward, his image sharpens, grows huge. He lays a coarse hand on her forehead. 'It's okay,' he says. 'The Chief here's a doctor – '

The Indian clears his throat.

'Well, kind of,' says her husband.

'A doctor?' she says, her blood suddenly pumping. 'Is there

something – ' She looks to the Indian who is shaking his head but still smiling. He pats her belly, welcomes the boy.

'The boy?' says my mama. 'You mean – '

He nods and my daddy nods too. The Chief looks down at her belly, somber like a son looking into a grave. Then, whispering, he says, 'In the name of the Great Spirit, Chief Yellowhammer welcomes you – '

At this my mama tries to speak but cannot. She looks at her new husband, for a moment clear-eyed, and knows in that moment that she doesn't love him, that he was just her escape, that she's made a mistake. He smiles at her. 'Darlin',' he says, his eyes filling with tears, 'ain't this the best news? Ain't it just the best?'

This, then, how it is this morning in my waking dream. In my dreams there are hands upon me, before I have hands of my own. Before I have eyes there are eyes upon me, and tears before I have tears of my own. In my dream I see Mama, feel the pumping of her blood, feel the life, now lost, spinning through her veins into mine. We are all one: this, surely, is the message of my dream. We carry, are carried. We are none of us alone.

The List

In case you've been thinking I never follow through on things, I can tell you here I've spent the last half-hour since getting back from Mama's grave compiling that list I mentioned. Right now I have fifteen things that need to get done or bought, and I'm sure there's more to come. Top of the list is of course food, followed by the phone to get connected and materials for the barn and then all sorts of other stuff, most of which occurred to me during my walk back across Salter's Field. It's amazing just what simple fresh air can do in the way of clearing your head. That and exercise I suppose – which is something that's been a little scarce around here lately. Walking around the house hardly counts, neither does all the traveling I've been doing in my head. Those kind of mind-miles – following Daddy's old Texas circuit or heading down through the Delta then west through Louisiana to the Gulf coast – seem to make you stiffen up rather than loosen you out, which for sure is not what I need. I mean I wake up these mornings and some mornings I can barely move. Some mornings it's like I've been walking all night, trudging through thick snow in waterlogged boots. But then the strange thing is that some mornings – like this morning first thing – though I'm weary like I've never been weary before I just can't stop walking and I find myself pacing this house, these rooms, and I find myself staring out over these fields just listening for the chock-chock of mallet on fencepost, just searching these noon fields for the slick trail of ghosts.

But, hey. It's that list that concerns me right now – upon which, in fifteenth and (so far) last place – just added – is bolts. I'm thinking two or three (maybe four to be on the safe side) should do it. Not that I'm expecting company you understand, it's just that it occurs to me that if I can get in here without a key then so can anybody else who happens to be passing. Not that anybody's likely to be passing – which is sort of the point. You see I figure if anybody does show up (not that I reckon, as I say, that they will, but, as the

Doctor used to say, you never can tell, and he was right), then for sure they must have been planning to be here and so you have to ask yourself why.

Hence those bolts, and this consequent feeling of unease.

For which, I see now, I can only blame Raymond.

It seems there are some things – fears especially – that you can never entirely get rid of, however hard you try to and however long you live. In my case, one such thing is Raymond B. Slimp. Raymond I was always frightened of when I was a boy and it seems I am frightened of him still. Just the mention of him even now and suddenly I'm that boy again, standing at that screen door in the first light of day, just waiting for the sight of him moving slow and steady down that dusty road and knowing that only the coming of dusk will see him heading back to his shack in the trees and that old army latrine and that part of his life I never even dared imagine. Just the thought of him and I can still see that stooping way he had of working and that way he had of looking at you like he was looking right through you and could see something coming that was bad. Even now all this – and why? Because of the wind playing tag in the trees and rattling the glass in these old wooden frames? Because of a few creaking floorboards? Jesus, I really must be going crazy. I mean I know it's all just echoes – just memories – don't I? – that what's past is past and done?

Well don't I?

I do – for sure.

And yet –

But no.

You're right. Staying calm is the thing. Not letting your mind run away. After all Raymond, we all know, is dead, and even if he did blame my daddy for taking his place here – for eating his food and for breathing his air and for sending him off to that jungle – well, so what? When you're dead you're dead and that's it. No comebacks. For sure no amount of echoes could ever change that.

12.15

Mystery Train

Whenever I consider the circumstances of my birth, it always strikes me as somewhat significant – given what has since occurred – that I should have made my debut appearance in this world one Saturday night at a little after eight, during Radio WXPM's live weekly broadcast from the Louisiana Hayride. It has long struck me also as further significant that my arrival up here in Creek County, Oklahoma, should have coincided exactly with the arrival down there on stage in New Orleans of Scotty Moore and Bill Black and their front man, Elvis Presley. You know to this day, whenever I hear 'That's All Right, Mama' or 'Mystery Train', the hairs on the back of my neck stand up and I think I hear (though I know in my heart this cannot be possible) my mama's screams, and I think I see – as I saw for the first time – the bright, blinding light of day.

You know it's a strange thing, but sometimes what, now, is really real to me is those things that I never really witnessed, but just drew in my mind from what I've been told. Like Mama for example at the gas-station window, and Daddy standing like a ghost on that forecourt. Then their first awkward talking, then their silences and so much more – even now I can hear it all, see it all, as clear as I'm seeing and hearing you now. In fact it's clearer to me now than those things I really saw, really heard – those things – reality – which seem sometimes no more than dreams – no more than the echo of some train in the darkness, no more than the brush of its passing on my cheek.

Ghost in the Latrine

Despite the noise of the TV I cannot shift Raymond from my
thoughts. I try to concentrate on the pictures, try to think of other
things but he's always there – standing in that way he had so still
that you'd think he was dead or sleeping even though his eyes
were open, or sometimes striding hard across that furthest field, his
arms held rigid by his side like they were tied and the tails of
his old winter coat dancing round his ankles like chickens on a
hotplate. Sometimes he's easing through the dusk at day's end, the
crunch of his boots in the dirt the only sound. Then the barn door
squeals and a light flicks on for a moment then off, then all's quiet
– a hush like a slow black tide rolling over the land, spreading
westward to California and the sea. Sometimes though he's just
lying in that jungle, his body festering, bugs crawling over him, his
eyes open and staring, accusing, his hands just a ghost's hands,
brittle and white against the darkness of his coat.

This coat.

Strange, I know, I should find it hanging still in the hall. After
all these years, with so much else gone, its presence has I admit
got me spooked again and led me to considering things it would
be best right now if I did not consider – things that should just be
let go – matters of guilt or otherwise – that no amount of turning
over the past could either confirm or once and for all deny. Which
of course doesn't stop me. Still I go on, endlessly squinting back
over my shoulder and searching for tracks that have long since
become obscured, transfixed by a footstep or the distant sound of
breathing, rocked into false dreams by the counterfeit touch of a
hand or the weave and weight of an old winter coat.

This coat.

His coat.

Surely it cannot be?

But a search of the collar says yes. *The Property of Raymond B.
Slimp*: here, his spidery writing, ink uncertain on cloth. I turn it,

dusty, hang it back on its hook. It settles, still, insolent and staring. Nothing but ghosts: these now are the lives in this house. I turn away, move slow through empty rooms. From this window the fields now are white, though only I know in memory, the shack and the old latrine out of sight but somehow in view, standing, leaning more than ever before, bleak against the white steaming field, the thin-boned arthritic trees. The latrine is coated heavy now with snow, dark slatted sides black in the fierce light. I step light, heel to toe, a boy again out for the rabbit traps, across the frozen stream, up the bank then on. The latrine draws close; I crunch on past, eyes fixed hard on the furthest tree, watching Larry's ramshackle deathtrap of a tree house hanging still, far off, caught like a kite in the skeleton branches.

Something then, whispering. I stop, turn, cock my head like a dog, listening.

'You ain't goin'?'

'I ain't goin'.'

'You gotta go.'

'Well I ain't.'

I ease myself over the hard ground, creep around the back of the latrine. I peer in through the slats. The wood is cool to my cheek.

'But you gotta.'

'I said I ain't goin' and I ain't.'

At first there's nothing to see – just darkness – then the gloom coalesces into shapes. A shape. A man, his eyes catching the slits of light, his head turning, growing suddenly larger. I step back, stumble on a root as the door swings open. I turn to run but my foot is caught, then there's hands on my shoulders, turning me back.

'What you doin'?'

His eyes look like thunder, gathered sharp, his fingers hard as claws in my flesh. He'll kill me I know, leave my body for the birds to pick clean.

'Huh? Well?'

'Nothing,' I say, but he's closer, his breath sour with whiskey, streaming out in white clouds.

'Ain't,' he says, breathing hard, 'ain't a man got no privacy? Can't a man get to talkin', get to conversing in peace?'

'But – ' The word just slips out, sharp and deadly. I brace for the cut.

'But what?'

But there's only you in there, says the voice in my head: I clench my teeth to keep it there. Over his shoulder the house is as tiny as a toy house, as far off and as unreachable as the moon. I close my eyes, there's a rushing in my ears, feel the sudden creeping warmth spreading slow down my thighs, hear it fizzle like a acid at my feet.

'He's awake.'

When at last I came to I was lying in my bed, anxious faces all around. I tried to push up, but could not. I lay back, eyes closing, drifted. In a sudden sharp dream I saw Daddy in the fields, riding a buffalo and hollering. Then my eyes were open and the figure was gone, replaced in the low light by faces: Mama, Aunt Celeste, Larry looking up to the ceiling, Daddy in his work clothes, blurred. Mama drifted towards me, a hand touched my face. 'Oh, Billy,' she whispered. I twisted on the pillow, thinking suddenly of Raymond. 'Is he going to the war?' I heard a voice saying, felt myself feeling the words in my throat. Mama's face folded in a frown; beyond her, Daddy, still blurred, looked down, slipped his hands in his pockets like a thief. Mama leaned forward, held my face in her hands. 'Sssh,' she whispered, 'Sssh now.' I opened my mouth to say something, but nothing came. All that came was silence, then a whistling in my ears, then the rolling far off of a distant muffled thunder, then gradually, growing nearer, rain.

Like this rain.

See it tap with tiny fingers on the window. See something changing in the sky. Hear distant footsteps running, splashing close by, fading.

Ghosts. Nothing in this house now but ghosts.

Jesus Christ.

Somehow I must rid myself of these paralyzing notions, before their grip has me good and I'm once and forever lost.

So.

Watch me smile, hear me talking. Watch me watching these flickering pictures; listen to that silence, just the soundtrack of rain. Christmas is coming: there's this message in the sky. Look away, look away; see it bruising, turning. Feel the shadows folding over these boots, this chair. Hear the sound of my singing. Christmas is coming. The future is mine. I must grasp it.

Circular World

The two things everybody knew in those days about Checker Noosefelt, Sheriff's Deputy, Comanche County, central Oklahoma, were, *a.* that his cousin Scoot had once nearly become one of Rickie Scallop's Seafood Serenaders, and, *b.* that Checker himself had a voice in song so deaf to tone that it was said to have once soured the milk of a cow called Valene. That he was singing to that cow in the first place (Elvis's 'I Want You, I Need You, I Love You', so the story has it), despite the best efforts of the beast's owner to prevent him, tells you in itself two further things about Checker Noosefelt. It tells you, *a.* that despite the overwhelming evidence to the contrary he considered his singing voice to be generally a thing of beauty and specifically beneficial to a milk-cow gone dry, and, *b.* that he was not a man to be easily deflected from his task. Addressed to his face as the Singing Deputy (as in, 'Hello, Singing Deputy, and how are you today?') and behind his back as the Tone-Deaf Deputy, it was Officer Noosefelt's voice (or so I am told) that was the first voice I ever heard – a fact which, given what has since occurred, I have reason both to celebrate and to deplore. Celebrate because it was, I believe, this voice, singing as it was (however poorly), that led me inexorably, through some powers so deep that they're way beyond my understanding, to that which I once called my career, and deplore for the very same reason. It was this, I believe, that led me to Audacity, and this that, in the end, led to Amarillo and her driving away and me following her – this that led me to that Arkansas hillside and then to my time at the Institute, and then to here, now. All of which merely goes to underline my belief that every true thing in this world is circular, and that where and how we entered so one day will we exit. Somebody once said that there is no journey that is not a journey home, and this is what I believe. I believe that from that first moment of life all of life is set; in my case, that it was Checker Noosefelt, with his voice ringing out through the house at the moment of my birth, who, for better or for worse, gave birth in later years to my so-called career, and set me on a path to here. Not that I'm blaming him you understand; I'm just saying.

Anyway.

That day.

Just what Checker Noosefelt was doing that day at the farm I have no idea, and little chance now of ever finding out. All I do know is that he was there and that it was just as well for everybody that he was, given the scenes that followed. You see, no sooner was I there – here – screaming and crying at the world and the injustice of being put through being born at all – than Daddy and Uncle Braxton were fighting. But then they were always fighting. From the start, like cats and dogs is what people used to say, and I guess that was right. Looking back, it was like it was some kind of natural hatred, something maybe peculiar to brothers, that only needed them being together and breathing the same air to make it explode. Anyway, that day they exploded – Uncle Braxton hurling insults and my daddy then hurling his fists, the result of which was Uncle Braxton (who was unstable enough on his one real leg at the best of times) falling over and out through an open window and on to Aunt Celeste's border of alpine blooms, a result that only made things worse. As a fight, I guess you could say it was a big one – in fact it might have been their last had Checker Noosefelt not stepped in when he did. With a hand on each chest (he was, as I've said, a big man and neither intimidated nor surprised by man's bad intentions toward man), he told them to hush up and directed their attention to the crying coming from above, saying they should be ashamed. Whether or not they were ashamed I have no idea (I doubt it), though they did – for a while at least – stop fighting. But only for a while. Soon they were back at it, sniping and cussing like two polecats in a bag, year after year until the day Daddy got in his pick-up and just drove away.

You know, thinking about it now, it amazes me that Daddy didn't go sooner, knowing what he knew and considering how long he knew it – that it took as long as it did for his feet to find the deck of that riverboat and his chest to feel that water's tightening embrace, and his eyes to see that darkness, then the blinding of eternity's light.

94

3.00

So Far So Good

Well three o'clock already and I've not thought of Raymond for nearly an hour, which is good. I mean for someone whose nature it is to dwell on things that would be best forgotten. Who knows, maybe soon there'll be nothing in my mind but positive forward-looking thoughts. Maybe soon I'll be out of here and driving down that highway, heading into town. Maybe soon I'll be back in the world – who knows?

3.45

The Weathergirls, They Lie

Jesus, I can't believe this rain. For hours now it's been beating on these windows and lashing real spiteful at the fields (not to mention spinning the TV aerial around on the roof and flickering my picture so bad it's hard to tell what the hell it is I'm watching), when all the time all I've been hearing about is that snow that's on its way (heading south, last I heard, through southern Minnesota and Iowa), and how, when it hits it's gonna be real bad. Well. So much for that. You know these days it seems you can trust nearly nobody. These days, some days, it seems all you've really got is yourself.

5.10

The Boxers

There's this picture that comes to me in dreams and increasingly these days during my waking hours. It's this: I'm ringside and there's these boxers and they're so exhausted through struggling that they're holding on to each other and hugging each other like they're lovers or something. Then suddenly the bell goes and it's the end of the fight and then just as suddenly there's only silence in the hall and the hall's empty, and it's just me sitting there and there's sweat on my brow. There are voices in the distance then, then nothing. I wake.

All of which means?

Maybe something, maybe nothing. Whatever. All I do know is those boxers weren't hugging 'cause they wanted to. They were hugging just to keep themselves standing, just to keep themselves from falling so far that they'd never in a lifetime get up again. Which, it occurs to me (and you know I've been thinking some more about Mama and Daddy), is maybe all any of us ever does. Maybe getting close is just some kind of defense – hanging on to somebody just a way of not getting hit.

Okay, you say, but what about love?

Okay, so maybe I'm wrong. Maybe not. All I know is that love is needing and needing's just searching for the means of survival – so what is love if not just hanging on – clinging on against the fear of falling, of nothing?

Like I say, I've been thinking some more about Mama and Daddy.

I suppose I knew right from the start that love isn't some soft kind of thing like summer clouds or a place by a creek in the shade, but something hard and brittle like some ladder made out of plaster that you climb up out of the jungle until it breaks and you're falling to the earth again, naked and sprawling. Leastways, this is what I was instructed. You see from the start I always knew from their looks that Mama and Daddy were just saving themselves – hanging on to each other as long as they could until they couldn't hang on any longer – and from the start I knew it was all going to end. That end was in the future of course – some day way way ahead – and it stayed that way until one day that future crept up and I was standing on that road watching Daddy raising stones from the wheels of his pick-up, then listening to the growl of his engine in the trees. *At last*, I remember thinking, *It's happened at last*, and there was something about it that made me let go my breath like I'd been holding it and holding it for so long that my chest would surely burst. And I can feel again the solid unmoving weight of my limbs and that buzzing in my ears of silence, then there's hands in my hands and Mama's face hanging low before mine. 'Billy?' she's saying, 'are you feeling alright?' I close my eyes tight, open them wide, watch her shaking in answer to my question. 'Of course not,' she says, 'not *forever*', but there's something in that shaking, something in her eyes, that reveals the lie. I try to smile – want to smile – but nothing comes. All that comes is that – this – silence, the casual thumping of my heart.

It was later that night, with Larry face down and snoring by my side, that the boxers first came to me in shallow even sleep. From ringside that night I watched them, eyes squinting in the light, as I have watched them so many times since. I felt that night as I still feel some nights their sweat drifting down like wet dust, heard as I still hear their muffled angry moans. They twist and turn in their vicious embrace as ever they do in my dreams. And in my dreams too I can see still their bloodless desperate hands, feel still their knuckles and fingers raking my flesh as they fall.

6.30

The Solution to the Problem

Well after all that looking, would you believe they've been here all the time – pressed flat inside a book of figures (farm accounts they look like, though it's difficult to tell, the writing being so sloping and the ink now so faded), right here amongst a pile of books on top of the piano and staring out at me like they've been willing me to find them and I've just been blind or careless or something, which – looking back now – I suppose I have.

Anyway.

Whatever.

At last, these plans.

You know reading them it seems like – as far as the structure is concerned – Stig's barn is in essence (like I suppose all barns) a very simple affair, made up basically of four wooden pillars, one at each corner, each of which is sunk into some sort of concrete base, each of which in turn is sunk into the earth to a depth of approximately fifteen feet. These pillars are then connected to each other by a network of beams and cross-beams which provide the structure with its lateral strength. The roof is constructed in the same way, then covered – as are the walls – with bolted-together sheets of treated ply. Today, though these sheets are a little buckled, I think they're in generally pretty good shape – as, as far as I could tell (I'm no engineer) are the pillars and beams. In fact such problems as there are seem not so much to do with the structure as with the hundreds of bolts that hold it all together – or don't as now seems to be the case. From what I have seen, it seems so many of them have somehow just got to be too small for their holes (God knows how), while some of them just aren't there at all. Which accounts, I suppose, for the barn's unsteadiness. Which in turn means that maybe all that needs to be done to keep the whole thing standing (though God knows what further damage this rain'll be doing) is to replace all the bolts and in so doing hopefully to strengthen things in time for this snowfall if it ever comes. Of course I realize this is no small job and that pretty much anybody else would be better qualified than me to undertake it, but when all you've got is yourself then, well, that's all you've got and you better make the best of it, 'cause for sure no one else will. Besides, what could be so tough about replacing a few old bolts? Is it surgery of the brain I'm talking about? It is not. Surely really all that's needed is the time (which right now at least I do have), the inclination (ditto sometimes), and of course maybe two or three hundred bolts, the getting of which being right now as I see it my only problem and only then due to my own shortcomings, chief amongst which so far has been this creeping unwillingness to move – particularly as far as Sayreville. Still, with the plans having been found now and consequently a new start for things beckoning, this is something that must be addressed, and just setting off – just going – is surely the best way to proceed. So all I need right now is a sudden rush of courage which I'm certain any minute will come.

10.17

Any Minute

Well as you can see I'm still waiting – still sitting right here with these plans on my knees and the day drifting by me like leaves on a slow-flowing river. Any minute, I keep thinking, Any minute, but the minutes just keep ticking on by and turning themselves into hours. Soon I know the day will be gone and again nothing will have been done. And then (for sure – I know it) that snow I've been dreading and praying for will come shooting across the sky, smothering the dawn then the land and busting that barn up real good and all the time I'll know it could have been saved. And then? Well Audacity of course, standing on that porch and me sitting here still unable to move or even sleeping. For sure in my dreams and then waking I'll hear her calling my name, then the sound of her footsteps growing faint in the yard. And then? Then nothing, just me – unless I push myself up right now, unless I pack up these plans and get going.

So.

Here I go.

Three.

Two.

One.

But then again. Look at that yard and those fields. Look how they're fading so fast into black. Maybe I should wait awhile, step out at first light. Bubba after all will have closed up the store hours ago – and besides, what if I lose my way? What if the road is not as I remember it? What if I stumble over roots long forgotten, or pitch myself into my old rusted traps? What then?

No, sir.

Good sense must in these circumstances prevail.

So. For the moment I shall sit tight, wait for first light, maybe sleep if sleep comes. Anyway, whatever, I shall wait now for tomorrow. Tomorrow, God willing, I shall begin my ascent.

Friday

Tomorrow Today Already

Woke to four bells, to the cold in this room. Already the sun is rising far off through the haze. I have tried to rise too, but cannot. Stiffness prevails. Unlimber limbs rebel, rigid now after night's adventures.

Dreams, I should say.

Memory.

The day, of course, of Daddy's leaving. I see it now, clear in dreams, how I ran from the house and over the yard, out past the well and on to a dirt road, my feet slapping hard in the dust. I recall how I stood then in the trees, looking down, how the figures in the yard stood still and watching, their tiny hands shielding their eyes. And I remember how I closed my eyes and how I opened them, and how for a moment there was nothing in the glare but whiteness, how the color bled back then and I turned, ran on, ran harder and harder, the ground rough on my feet, until, heaving, nearly retching, I stood in the dusk, squinting up at a sign in the gloom: LEAVING CLARK COUNTY – COME BACK SOON! I remember it all as clear as day – how the road up ahead took to shifting, how the trees lost their sharpness in the gathering dusk. Clear as day now I can feel my heart thumping, hear the giveaway click in my throat as I swallow. Faces loom in the darkness, leering, then recede. Then I'm turning again as I turned, running blind again, feeling again the pain of running, on and on, so hard that I'm sure I will die. All comes back to me now, clear in perfect memory. It was, I see now, the start of the running that led me here, to sitting here silent and waiting for snow.

But again I digress.

Back to that day.

When finally I fell I fell hard and lay where I fell, the strength seeping from my body like blood through my chest, my cheek grinding stones on the cool damp earth, my eyes closed tight for fear of what I'd see.

A voice then suddenly, far off but getting nearer. I shut down my ears, covered them with my hands, filled my throat with humming as I prayed to sweet Jesus to let me be home – to let me be lying again in the room I'd so foolishly abandoned, let the morning again rise gold through the curtains, let Mama be there and I swear I'll never ever do such a fool thing again, sweet Jesus, oh, sweet Jesus –

A hand gripped my shoulder then, the curl of strong fingers. 'Well now,' said the voice (it was up close now), 'what in Beelzebub are you doin' out here, Billy-Boy?'

I froze. Billy-Boy? The stranger knew my name?

I squinted through slits: the silhouette of boots, dark in the searing white of headlights.

'Well, Billy-Boy, ain't you got no tongue?'

'Leave me alone,' I said. My voice was shaking. I heard it say my daddy'd be there any minute.

'Your daddy?'

'And he'll kill you!' I said.

'Kill me? Now why in heaven would your daddy want to be doin' somethin' like that?'

'Because he's mean!'

'Mean, huh?'

'And he'll, he'll – '

'He'll what, Billy-Boy? What exactly's old Glenn gonna do?'

My heart skipped a beat. I opened my eyes. The figure was dark, in shadow. 'How'd you know my daddy's name?' I said.

'Old Glenn? Well shoot, boy, me and your daddy's been buddies since, well, since the day you all arrived – '

Buddies? I pushed myself up, squinting hard through the dark. 'Who are you?' I said, but in the moment of speaking I saw who it was. 'Singing Deputy?'

'You got it, boy!'

Checker Noosefelt cracked a smile; as soon as it had come, though, it was gone. He frowned. 'Say Billy,' he said, 'you ain't really waiting on your daddy – are you?'

'I am!'

He held up his palms. 'Okay, okay – ' The frown softened into puzzlement. 'Look – ' he started then, but I cut him off. My daddy, I said, was headed for Texas.

'Texas?'

'Uh-huh,' I said.

Checker opened his mouth to speak, but changed his mind. He was studying me hard; my eyes slid from his. In the end he said, 'What about your mama?'

I shrugged. A hand touched my shoulder. Checker Noosefelt dropped to his haunches, tipped back his sheriff's hat. 'Where's he gone, son?' he said, 'your daddy – '

I told him the circuit.

'The circuit?'

And I told him how he'd be back, but hearing the words spoken just confirmed what I knew in my heart: that it was untrue, that he'd never be back, that it was just my mama's hopeless lie.

Checker Noosefelt whistled low. He took off his hat and drew his fingers through his sparse hair. For a second his face caught the lights from his car; his flesh in that moment was shiny, grayish-looking, the sharp bottom edge of his mustache wet with sweat or dew. He replaced his hat, set it firm. He stood; he was suddenly a mountain. 'Hey, kid,' he said, 'what d'you say me and you take a ride, huh?'

I shrugged.

'Look,' he said. He paused; I looked up. There was something in his eye – a look that was almost like guilt – and I knew by that look that he knew the truth. I looked away, out to the gloom, the trees beyond. The night was still, there were fireflies in the trees.

We drove in silence, save for the voices on the radio. I stared through the window at the black empty night – at myself looking palely back. With every mile that passed by I felt my daddy sitting somewhere in some room and waiting, and with every mile, the flick of every telegraph pole, I could see him watching me making a choice. I thought of him lying on his bed in some motel, squinting in the lamplight at his watch and waiting, and I knew that by then he'd know I'd made my choice. I saw him reaching over and twisting off the light, and in the darkness of that car moving south along the highway, a cool dense guilt settled heavy on my shoulders. *And now Patsy Cline*, whispered the voice of the Hossman on the radio. *Crazy,* she sang as I stared at myself, at my child's hateful face, and, with the road running backwards away away, I felt myself glowing with the shame of desertion.

It was rising dawn when we turned off the highway and started down the track. The house was blaring light through uncurtained windows, smoke rising lazy from the stack. We crunched to a halt in the yard.

The Deputy cut the engine. He touched the horn. Nothing. 'Guess they're all out searching, huh?' he said. I shrugged. He opened his door and stepped out.

We were sitting in the parlor, the Deputy chasing songs through the radio static, when I heard Uncle Braxton pulling up. A car door, then another, opened and slammed. Footsteps in the dirt then, the screen door banging. I knew I should stand, do something, be glad at least to be home and safe, but I couldn't. Instead I sat there rigid – aware of something missing, gone forever – seeing only the bitter face of my daddy abandoned, hearing only the sad voice of the Deputy hit a note so unexpectedly clear and true that it startled even the crows roosting high in the eaves and sent them spinning, fanning out, black as tacks thrown up against the pale autumn sky.

6.35

Elk City Blues

One letter in the mailbox from yesterday, and I don't have to have X-ray eyes to know who it's from. For one thing there's the writing – how it slopes like a drunk first this way then that and barely gets to get joined up at all – and for another there's this stamp on the back: *Life's Better In Elk City,* above what I first thought was some kind of picture of the world but which I see now is just a smiling face. Also, I don't need those special eyes to know what it says inside. For sure it'll be more of the same pleading, more of the same talk about Christmas. *Don't you know it's a time for family?* he'll say, or maybe just, *Don't forget I'm your brother.* As usual, what he'll conveniently forget is that if anybody's deserting anybody around here then it's him that's deserting me by doing something so dumb as what he did in the first place and getting himself arrested in the second – not to mention the little fact that we're only half-brothers anyway, which has to make a difference. And besides, it's not as if we were ever really close; in fact, truth to tell, I always knew he was dumb and would wind up one day where he has wound up, even when we were trailing around together and having races in the dust or building things together like real brothers are supposed to. I couldn't have said exactly what he'd do (even I could never have imagined anything quite as dumb as this Elk City fiasco), just that I knew he'd do something and that for sure he'd get caught, which he has many times. Just how many times I couldn't say. All I could say is I reckon that if you counted up all the days dear Larry has spent behind bars of one kind or another then they'd make up the majority of all the days of his life. And the worst thing is that it's not just his own time he's wasted: I mean how many days over the years have I wasted sitting the other side of that piece of thick glass just listening to his whining, or just scrabbling around trying to make up his bail? Don't ask is how many. And now? Now he writes me in that dumb sloping hand of his, whining about how it's Christmas and we're brothers and how I have to go see him just one more time. *I'll be better this time*, he'll say, *I won't fool around*. Well sure. Some chance. Fooling around was always just about the only thing he was ever any good at. I mean, Jesus. How dumb can you get? He can't even get himself caught doing some regular kind of crime. No, sir. Not Larry. He has to do something so stupid that it makes the national news – and not even the headlines, mind, but as one of those winding-up let's-cheer-'em-up-after-all-this-bad-news items – an appearance that makes him what he thinks is some kind of hero but which in fact just means he's stupid and everybody knows it. So he gets letters. So what? So what if there's women out there that say they're in love with him and send him their pictures and all kinds of other stuff – what does that prove? What it proves is there's a whole bunch of sad individuals out there, the contemplating of which is enough to drive a person to some kind of despair. America. Land of the Free. Oh sure. Home of the Brave. You know sometimes it seems like this whole nation's gone crazy. Sometimes I can't help thinking that we must have gone wrong somewhere – taken the wrong road way back someplace. Sometimes I think we're heading for sure for disaster, that I'll wake up one morning to find every-thing gone – to just shadows on the land where there used to be houses and silence where there used to be birdsong. There'll be nothing to show then we were any good at all – just air so foul it'd kill you to breathe it and soil that's thin and exhausted – just a blighted barren land that was once so bountiful – just seas, now poisoned, that were once rich with life. America, America. Last great hope. How in God's name could we have done what we've done?

But steady now.

Getting carried away doesn't help. Whatever the future, it is just a whole bunch of todays end to end. So. Today. This letter. For now I shall put it aside, maybe look at it later. Right now there's that trip into town to take. Right now there's that car to get started.

I Should Have Known

Well of course I should have known. Should have guessed it. Three weeks without moving and the battery in the Doctor's old Pinto was sure to be flat, which it is. Just the insolent click of the starter, then nothing. Silence. Which of course explains why I'm back here so soon – why, instead of being halfway to town by now, maybe talking with Bubba at the store, I'm sitting here at Mama's old kitchen table with nothing having changed, except the rain. The rain having stopped I suppose is something. Maybe at last there'll be some chance of that snow. Which, of course, in turn, makes the trip all the more urgent, which is not something I can think about right now, there being nothing right now I can do about it. I have the battery on charge in the pantry and that's it. There's nothing more I can do, except wait. Watch TV maybe, maybe answer the other letter I found this morning jammed in back of the mailbox behind Larry's. How long it's been sitting there I don't know. There's no date on it and the postmark's so faded now it's imposs-ible to make it out. All there is is upright childish writing – *Dear Mr Songhurst, I'm writing to ask you* – the loops and curls of some-thing rough copied out. Signed Katie Platt, there's a sadness about it, something touching in its distant and unknowing concern for somebody that's now dead – a call that demands an answer.

Anyway, while I'm waiting for that battery, let me read it:

Dear Mr Songhurst,
I'm writing to ask you if Louie's OK because when Emma (she's my sister) and me saw him he was sick. Is he better now? I hope so.

> Signed,
> Katie Platt (aged 8)

Well, Jesus, it's weird how things can take you back – how a few faded words on a page can call up a whole certain past. Not for years have I let myself think of those times – of Louie in his first years with us and how the fever that made Uncle Braxton mail his leg off to Washington nearly killed Louie it gripped him so bad, and how even, when at last the worst of it was past, it left a look in that bird's eye that he never did lose – not even, years later, when he lay, in death, in the trunk of my car. I mean even then, when he lay quite still and so old, there was something about him that made you think he was watching – how, old as he was and dead as he was, chances were any second he'd be out of there, wings thrashing and stabbing with that beak of his, as mean in death as ever he had been in life, which I can tell you at times was real mean – so mean in fact that even Gilber Creek who'd introduced him to the farm in the first place sometimes refused to step into that barn alone, so wary was he of that bird's unpredictable nature. In fact, in the weeks before I left the farm after Uncle Braxton's funeral it was only me that went near him at all, and even with me he was always in one sour mood. Of course it was me or nobody – which, it occurs to me now – he maybe sensed. Maybe he knew that, with Uncle Braxton gone, the family was finally so broken that nothing could ever stitch it back together again – that with Larry in jail (again) and Aunt Celeste murmuring in some rest home upstate, not to mention Mama turning away any help that might save her this farm, and me with my bags packed and the keys to Uncle Braxton's old Dodge in my hand – that what had seemed once immovable, as solid as the trees and the very earth at our feet, was in the end just as fragile and fleeting as the last leaves of summer or the first mild days of winter. Maybe he knew; maybe he didn't. I don't know. All I do know is that there was something like bitterness or hopelessness or something in his eyes as I raised up that shotgun and tried to take aim. I squinted, looked away, rubbed my eyes, looked back. I drew my breath and held it, squeezed on those triggers.

But of course I couldn't do it. Not me. I couldn't even finish off some crazy old liability of a bird, couldn't take my revenge for Uncle Braxton. No. I just stood there, staring down, knowing as I did so that however long I stood there, however hard I tried, that I was never going to do it, never break free.

So?

So, with a heaviness of heart I have seldom felt since, I uncocked that shotgun and took that old bird on the road.

10.00

Serve Her Right

So three hours that battery's been charging now, which I'm assuming is not enough, although of course just looking at the thing sitting there humming in the pantry, it's impossible to tell. My guess is that it still has some way to go. At the moment I'm thinking maybe noon for the off – one at the latest. That way, all things going as they could, I could maybe get into town and back by three. Of course I shall have to leave a note just in case, which I shall attach somehow to the door. And if Audacity should come by during the time I'm away? Well she'll just have to wait. In fact, a part of me's now hoping that she's standing there when I get back, waiting for me in the way I've been waiting so long for her. Right now I feel there would be about that a kind of symmetry that's pleasing – you could even say it would serve her right, pay her back some maybe for all the harm she's done to this heart. I mean, Jesus. Haven't I waited and worried more than a grown man should? Shouldn't I – by now – be calm in the darkness and not waiting every moment for a hand to come soothe me? Certainly I should. A thirty-five-year-old child is sometimes what I think I am. Sometimes I think maybe these last twenty years never happened at all – that maybe I was dreaming all those years and miles, and that at any moment now I'll just open my eyes and all that's happened will be yet to happen – all of which of course is just so much rambling and is getting me no place at all. I shouldn't be thinking like this right now. What I need to be doing right now is getting myself ready for the trip, maybe writing that note.

So.

What do I need?

For the note, some paper and something to write with.

But write what exactly?

This is going to need some thought.

Hmmm.

Something just occurred to me.

Did I mention Mama's vase was cracked? Split into two like it was made out of plaster and someone took a knife to it? Well it is, which – it occurs to me now – it being a consequence of this drop in temperature to near damn freezing it feels like (itself a result of that rain moving south into Texas) – is not going to be helping this battery situation one bit. You do not after all have to be any kind of a genius to know that real cold weather and the ability of batteries to hold a charge do not go well together. In fact, I'm thinking right now that, unless I do something, then that battery might never get charged sufficiently at all and I'll be stuck here until Easter maybe or until they find me and take me away.

But do what?

Well as I see it now there's only one thing, which is to heat up this house – particularly right now the pantry. Which means of course getting up and heading down to that basement and somehow getting that old furnace going. It's only my laziness I guess that's stopped me doing something about it before. Now, though, it seems I have no choice. It's start the thing up or nothing – no heat (and, Jesus, it is getting cold), no battery, no battery no Pinto, no Pinto no trip into town. And no trip into town? Well, no trip means just sitting here waiting, just watching that snow which is surely now on its way – just look at the weight in the whiteness of that sky – and how it'll lean on that old barn until the barn's all gone and my mission (for such now does it seem) is just another to have ended in failure.

So.

The furnace it is.

And, yes, don't think I don't know what you're thinking. You're thinking, will he ever get going? Will he ever get to town? Oh, still, how little you know me. When since you've known me have I ever looked for reasons not to move? When in these last weeks (or indeed in these last years) have I ever let fear of what's coming dim my courage, or the grip of the past slow my stride?

Down in the Jungle Room with Elvis

Well here I am at last. I say at last because negotiating my way through the house and down those steps was just about as difficult as I guessed it would be. It's partly the cold of course, but mainly (and this I'm admitting, okay, so don't give me a hard time) it's the drinking. This drinking is something I know I'll have to cut out, especially before noon. Which I can tell you will not be easy – especially with this sudden cold. I really don't know what in the world's happened. All of a sudden it seems the winter's come on real strong. You know it's got so cold now the windows are starting to blur up – so cold my breathing's started pouring out of me like smoke from some stack.

All of which of course – this cold – is why I'm here.

So get on with it.

Okay.

The furnace then.

You know it wasn't until I actually got down here (having nearly, in the process, broken my neck on these wooden steps that always were rickety but now are a whole lot worse) that that whole business about replacing the boiler came back to me. Or not replacing it I should say, the money to buy a new one being Uncle Braxton's and therefore too hard come by to be wasted on things we already had. The fact that even then this old one was so hungry for wood that barely a day went by when it didn't need stoking didn't come into it. If it ain't broke and all that. Talk about a false economy. Of course everybody knew the real reason was because the idea for replacing it (by some new self-charging or something electrical furnace) came first from my daddy and therefore was bound to be no good and something that wouldn't get done in a month of Sundays even if the likelihood of us all freezing to death was one hundred per cent dead cert. Of course there was arguing, but everybody might just as well have kept their mouths shut. Once Uncle Braxton decided on something there was no shifting him –

especially if that something involved my daddy. 'No, sir,' he'd say, and that would be that – which 'I'm-the-boss-here-and-don't-you-forget-it' tone just served to make things a whole lot worse, and would lead in turn to more cussing and fighting. Sometimes I used to sit down here in the dark just listening to the two of them shouting somewhere in the house or maybe out in the yard, and I used to think it was almost as if they couldn't get by without shouting – like they needed each other like those boxers in my dream. I'd squeeze down, listening, for hour after hour it seemed like, drifting off sometimes to the rhythm of their shouting. Then I'd wake from some dream and for a moment not dare to move in the sudden silence. One day, I recall, a whole day passed by in dreaming – dreams of Elvis and the Jungle Room and our sitting together playing tunes on some shiny black piano. All around us were chairs and tables carved in one piece from the trunks of huge trees and thick brown carpet on the ceiling and blue and purple feathers and water running down the far wall and into a pond filled with lilies and fish. We were singing gospel songs – 'How Great Thou Art', 'His Hand in Mine', 'I'm Gonna Walk dem Golden Stairs' – trading verses and laughing, caught up, the two of us, in the joy of just singing. For hour after hour we sang, pausing some-times to pour lemonade from a pitcher and feel it running cold as silver down our throats. Now and then there'd be moments of silence between songs and I'd watch his face, studying, without being seen, as he turned a page or laid his fingers on the keys as careful as a blindman. I'd study his hair, so black it would some-times catch blue in the light, and his nose that was as straight as my own. Then he'd sing out and play, his eyes closed in worship and I'd feel my heart filling with love.

That evening, waking from my dream, I knew something other than sleep had occurred. I knew in that moment, as my eyes fought the darkness and my limbs cried out in pain, that something had been shown to me – something that, if only I could see it, would change my life – but what? I studied the darkness for clues, closed my eyes tight, tried to go back but could not. And all the time beside me the furnace ground on, ripping through pine with its vicious iron jaws and spitting out sparks that rose, burned and died against the blue-black winter sky.

That evening, I recall, sometime around duskfall, I heard a truck pulling up in the yard, then Uncle Braxton calling out, 'Hey, Billy – you there, boy?'

I froze in my hidy-hole, shut down my breathing. More voices then – Mama's now – drifting through the night air: 'Billy – can you hear me, son?' Footsteps then, overhead, the creaking of boards, then silence, the opening of a door. Light for a moment flooded the basement.

'Billy – you down there?'

The sound of breathing then, then the closing of a door, then darkness, footsteps receding.

It was next morning, early, before anyone else was awake, that I took my first look at Louie. He was still in his crate just inside the barn door, head cocked and peering as I peered in at him. He growled. I stepped back. I'd never known a goose to growl. I stepped forward, was just reaching out, when a voice from behind me told me no and I turned.

Gilber Creek had his hands in his overalls, the lips in his thin face pulled back in a grin over stumpy yellow teeth.

'You ain't wanna do that,' he said. There was egg on his chin, yoke yellow-orange against his white-spattered overalls.

'What's he doing here?' I said.

Gilber Creek pulled off his cap. This, as ever, was paint-spattered too. 'Well,' he said. He looked down at his boots as if he were studying one of his fake painted cattle-grids, then scuffed them in the dirt, squinting at them as if they were somebody else's and something of a troubling surprise. 'Well,' he said, 'your daddy – '

My heart skipped. 'My daddy?'

He looked up. 'I mean with him bein', well, gone now an all – ' Gilber Creek cleared his throat. 'Well, see, your Uncle Braxton thought, well, you might be needin' some company – '

I felt my blood cooling, my heart-rate dropping down.

'And, well, me working up there on old Gill's place, and him with all them birds – '

I felt myself turning, looking into the crate. *What with your daddy bein' gone.*

'Say, Billy – you okay, boy?'

In my mind's eye, suddenly, I could see Daddy, but blurry, then

119

Uncle Braxton sharp in his chair and laughing. He was filling his pipe, his shoulders moving in his shirt.

'Son? You okay?'

I turned, walked slow, then faster, out of that barn, was running soon way out across the fields, into the cool of the trees. Here I slowed, doubled over, dry-retching. I dropped to my knees, felt the cool of the earth beneath my palms. *With your daddy bein' gone now.* I covered my ears, pressed them tight to my head, until all I could hear was the rushing of my blood and the echo of music in the trees.

6.00

Canary in a Coalmine

According to Bubba (and Bubba should know), Holly here is a bird with much potential. She is, he says, special – although exactly how (aside of course from the yellowness of her feathers and the sweetness – can you hear it? – of her song) he said he wasn't at liberty to divulge. You'll see, was all he'd say, You'll see, and that was that. No amount of coaxing from me would make him spit it out, which of course – having the nature I have – was enough to get me mad as hell, and is responsible for my having done what I recently did. Not, of course, that I'm saying he really deserved it – just that such selfishness, such unwillingness to tell the truth – is pretty much guaranteed not to be helpful in these kind of situations and that if you live and learn at all then you really should know this or look out. Anyway, I guess if you said what's done is done and there's nothing we can do about it then you'd be just about bang on the money – although this, of course, having, as I said, the nature I have, didn't stop me turning the whole thing over and over in my mind on the way home – replaying, if you like, the whole scene – until I got to wondering whether if maybe I couldn't just have bitten my tongue or held my breath or something and not said and done the things I did.

Anyway.

As you say, what's done is done and can't be undone. The important thing now is to move on – to do here, now, what must be done. There really is no point in making such a song and dance about it. That I can leave to Holly here. Singing and dancing is something she's real good at. Mind you, put me on a hotplate and I guess I'd be singing and dancing too.

6.20

Dusk Rises

I was reminded on my way home this evening of how, as a child, I used to believe that the dusk when it comes doesn't fall but it rises – that it creeps out of the fields and the creeks and then rolls slow-tumbling, hugging close to the land, until everything's gone and suddenly it's night. Of course it was just a child's foolish notion (the dusk, after all, neither rises nor falls, it just is, it just comes), although one, it appears, I have to this day not entirely managed to dismiss from my mind. Even today it is with me as strongly as ever it was – this feeling of being crept up on, encircled – to an extent that I have to admit has come as something of a surprise. In fact, earlier this evening it was nearly responsible for my being involved in an accident at the wheel of the Doctor's old Pinto. Of course, what with the events of earlier being fresh still in my mind (not to mention Holly here making something of a racket in her cage in its box in back) I suppose I was to a certain degree already on edge and ripe, you could say, for the attentions of spooks from the past. I guess you could say I was ready for Raymond to come lunging out of the dusklight, that old coat of his flapping round his ankles and a look on his face like he'd been waiting for me with some real bad intentions in his mind. Of course the suddenness (not to say unexpectedness) of his being there made me swerve something awful and made me think in those long seconds while I was spinning and that wheel was turning like it was greased through my hands of all kinds of stuff that I have not thought about in months and years – the kind of stuff I guess that a person only gets to thinking about when it seems like thinking's nearly through. There was Dougie Fishbein and Gilber Creek and Doctor Lark in his old two-tone Chrysler Fairmile. Before my eyes in those seconds there he was again, the Doctor, peering over the wheel of that beat-up old car, his hands stuck so tight through concentrating to that wheel that when he finally pulled up and got out, the wheel – leather-bound as it was – still had the dents in it where his fingers had been. And then he was gone, replaced as I recall by Experience at the Institute, by the turn of her hair as it wound its way up into clips and the scent of her starched white gown. *Lucky to be alive,* she was saying, that trace of a lisp in her voice; then she too was gone and everything was still – just the sound of my breathing and the frantic beating of my heart disturbing the silence, just the cool of the wheel in my hands. I went to open my eyes, but found them already open. I peered through the windshield, out into the dusk. Lucky to be alive, lucky to be alive. In the silence there was no one – just me on that road.

Just me and Holly that is.

In a while I twisted that key, drove on. I drove slow like I was steering that thing through a bustling crowd, staring out at the evening and waiting for the marker of the trees. When they came I turned even, felt the tires spitting stones and roll on. For a second my heart leapt at the lights in the window, but then I remembered. I thought of this note and knew in the moment of thinking that for sure it would still be where I'd left it, which of course it was. I drew to a stop, cut the engine. My hands were trembling as I opened the door.

That, now, an hour ago. Since then I've been standing here just watching the night coming on, just waiting for these echoes in my head to fade and this trembling in my hands to cease.

Coming Down

I have just completed a search of the car and can report with some relief that (as far as I can tell in this gloom) no damage was sustained as a result of the incident earlier on the road. It seems that where I was sure I had struck perhaps a tree in my swerving or even some kind of small creature I had in fact done no such thing – that the hit (a thump, I recall, followed by a scratching and tearing sound like branches or claws tearing at the vehicle's flanks) existed only in my imagination, and was itself – it seems likely – just a further consequence of my already by then heightened state of anxiety – a state from which I have yet entirely to recover. Indeed, even now, with some hours having passed, it's true to say that my hands still bear the traces of their shaking – a situation which (along with this still extra-hard beating of my heart) I shall have to do something about and soon if I am to make that start tonight as promised on the barn.

So. You'll excuse me if I just close my eyes for a while, maybe try to grab a little rest after all the exertions of the day. I don't, to be honest, have any great expectations of sleep – sleep as it does coming hard these days – although there is about my limbs a certain heaviness which is encouraging, a result no doubt of the day's unaccustomed physical activity.

So then, one minute and I'm gone. Before I do though, there is one other little thing that I feel inclined to say – something that has been bothering me since my return. You will have noticed that I have said nothing about that doubt I know for a fact was in your mind as to whether this trip just completed would ever in fact get made. Well, all I can say is shame on you for doubting me – although I do feel in all fairness I should also say that in the matter of doubting Billy Songhurst you are not alone. Bubba too this evening had that same look in his eye, as have others before him. Now, just why it exists in people I don't know, and right now I am far too tired to speculate. Right now I shall just sit here quiet, gather my thoughts perhaps – maybe watch a little TV – rest up a little anyway before beginning the evening's work.

7·35

My Favorite Show on TV

Well first reports as they say are encouraging. It seems (and here I have to admit a degree of surprise) that the bolts I was supplied with – those which caused Bubba such a struggle to find and which sat so heavy in the trunk of the car (and so contributed, it occurs to me now, to the enthusiastic way the car took to swerving when it started) are indeed the right size, just as he said they would be. I guess they're just some kind of standard barn size or something; anyway, whatever, they're the ones. Once you've got the old ones out (some of them come real easy while some – those that have rusted worst – take some knocking out with a hammer), getting the new ones in is in no way as hard as I thought it might be – a situation which has led me to these current feelings of optimism. Of course I know things could still go wrong (I'm not looking at the sky for fear the sky might be looking at me and might take my staring as a challenge to snow), particularly as so far I've managed to replace only a very tiny percentage of the bolts that are going to need replacing if the barn is to be saved. I would have done more had I not started so late and had I thought to take the ladder out with me, without which I only managed to do the ones I could reach, starting with those connecting the panels at what I still think of as Louie's corner. (It was there – at the corner furthest diagonally from the door – that Gilber Creek first set his box down and where after that Louie did all of his entertaining.) Anyway, as I say, I didn't get much done tonight, although making a start I feel after all this time is something. Who knows, an early start tomorrow and maybe I'll get the job done. Maybe by this time tomorrow I'll be able to look out this window without worrying about the weather – in fact with nothing but Audacity's arrival to worry about.

Which reminds me.

Jesus – will you look at the time? Here I am going on and on about how well I've done today – getting so carried away with bolts and such like – that I nearly missed *Blossom* on the TV. And to think, today is the day that Joey leaves for college and I nearly missed it. Jesus Christ. You know sometimes these days I just don't know what to make of myself. Sometimes I really feel I could be losing my grip.

8.30

Bereft

So he's gone. The end of an era. For a while there I thought maybe he'd turn back at the last minute, but no. It's a lesson I suppose, something to learn. Everything changes: something like that. Nothing in my heart I didn't really know of course, although, even so, having it confirmed like that – having Joey just walk out like that with everybody watching him like he was going off to war or something – still had an effect, still, I'll admit, took something of a shine off the day, leaving me now as you see me a little flat. It won't last of course. There is, after all, always tomorrow. Who knows, maybe in tomorrow's show we'll discover it was all just a dream – that Joey didn't really leave for college at all, that he was just fooling around – and that everything can go back to the way it was. Somehow I doubt it though. In the back of my mind I can't help thinking we've seen the last of Joey Russo: there was something so final in the way he closed that door.

But still, as you say, it's just a show. It's not as if it's real life. In real life when people step out they're gone. In real life you find yourself standing in the glare of some parking lot, listening like a fool to the growl of an engine till it's gone. In real life it's always raining, the rain falling heavy on your face. In real life people go and stay gone. In real life they never come back.

8.35

The Remains of the Day

The rain sweeping down, bright in the shaft of the parking-lot lights, the sickness of losing in my stomach: this and Audacity, the growl of a Firebird growing faint – my memory tonight of that day. Tonight as ever that day is close – three months, three minutes, three seconds; tonight as ever there is nothing I can do. I call out, but the rain takes my words; I run, but the road drains my strength. Then I'm standing, the rain lashing my face, the hot breath of trucks on my cheek.

'You're joking, right?'

How grotesque it seems now, that hard mocking tone in my voice. Why could I not have just smiled? A smile costs nothing and can gain so much. But no. My voice rising sharp against the rhythm of the band, the words come spitting out. 'It's a joke, right?' I say, though I know in that moment of speaking it's no joke, that it's starting again, that the handing-on's begun.

She shakes her head, looks down, up sharp. 'So what are you saying?' she says, her voice just a whisper lost against Bitter Pete's guitar. Trying to think of nothing, I just shake my head, turn away. Out front, a carpet of faces, upturned, like a field of summer flowers by moonlight. I turn back; she's gone. Is gone still.

Which brings me to tonight, to now. Looking out at this darkness I can't help wondering where she is right now, and whether (dare I even think it?) she's out there close maybe, maybe headed my way, maybe cruising right now down Sayreville's sleeping Main Street, pausing perhaps outside Bubba's store and peering in, or maybe she's sitting at the top of the rise, squinting down at the lure of this lamp.

Maybe.

But I doubt it.

Besides, the remains of that day are telling me no. Even from here – from now, tonight – even with the blurring of sleep coming on – there is something so final in the rasp of that engine as it dies, something so permanent – so forever and ever – in the weight of that slow-rising silence.

Saturday

6.15

On the Eve of Christmas

Waking hungry this morning from my usual dreams of flight, I am reminded, lying here, that today is a day of homecoming feasts. Today, all over America (and I guess all over the world), trains are being boarded and cars started up; all over the country (all over the world) people are hurrying home, their heads full of stories and their bags full of gifts as yet unwrapped. Lights wink on electrically in trees across the nation and trash sits forgotten out back. A dog barks, alerted by something in the air; a voice rises, falls away, then a screen door bangs. Christmas is coming, another year turning.

I turn in Mama's bed, stare up at the ceiling. Laziness draws up and over me like a blanket, settles heavy on my limbs. I must rise, though, for there is much to do. On this, the eve of Christmas, I too have plans. I too have preparations to make.

6.30

Holly and Ivy

I refuse to feel guilty as conscience suggests I should about taking Bubba's food. It is, after all, of no use to him, and besides, to leave it would have been to waste it. Of course you could say that perhaps I should not have taken it in the first place – but that's another matter. To get into that would be to get into all kinds of questions of right and wrong which would involve all kinds of explanations for which right now I have neither the time nor the inclination. Right now all I'll say on the subject is that you were not there and do not know. So please, do not judge me. Watch me eat if you must – but do not speak. There has been altogether too much talking around here lately – a situation which, everybody knows, is the enemy of the working man. Which – this morning at least – is what I am. This morning, once breakfast is done and cleaned away, I shall pull on Raymond's old working boots once more and his gloves and continue – and hopefully complete – my work on the barn. That done, I shall go fetch some more wood for the furnace and maybe check on that battery. In this kind of cold – where batteries are concerned – I believe you cannot be too careful.

So then.

Breakfast.

First though – before I start – a word about Holly, about whom I know you have shown some concern. Okay. Two points. Point one is that, although I did not choose her I was obliged to take her, seeing as how she was a gift, and so, if I blunder in the looking after of her, well, blame Bubba not me. Point two has to do with her dancing. Cruel, you say, having her dancing on that hotplate. Well I agree. However, Bubba's the expert and he said no. He said (and this is no word of a lie) to deprive that bird of the opportunity to perform would be to kill it as surely as if you just went and stepped on it. How so? you say, as I did. Well, turns out Holly here was once part of a show that Bubba and his daddy used to take every year on the county fair circuit – 'Big Beak Biloxi and his

Beautiful Birds', the show was called – a show that got to be so famous that they even performed one time (this is according to Bubba) before the Governor and his wife at the state fair in Oklahoma City. According to Bubba, the stars of the show were Holly and Ivy, who, he said, were billed – due to the daredevil nature of their performance – as the Thelma and Louise of the canary world. It seems – aside from the tricks they could perform while dancing like yellow maniacs on a pair of matching hotplates – the mainstay of their act involved Ivy getting shot from some kind of miniature cannon while Holly chirped 'Hail to the Chief'. Though wildly successful, causing as it did spectators to be able to hail both the American can-do-ness of the world's greatest performing canaries and the office of President in one go, it was this part of the act which apparently led to its downfall. Now, Bubba's daddy, it seems, liked to take a drink (said it steadied his hand) – although never ever before a show. Except of course that one tragic time. Learning two minutes before commencing that state fair performance that his wife – Bubba's mama – had run off with a dry-walling contractor from New Jersey (a man who, apparently, due to an incident earlier in life had virtually no nose at all – a fact which may or may not have been significant in Bubba's daddy's distress) Bubba's daddy fell headlong for solace into a bottle of bourbon – an act for which the consequences, both for himself and for his stars, meant disaster, for not only did his subsequently inaccurate targeting of the cannon result in Ivy's unfortunate assault on the person of the state's First Lady (which caused, in its turn, due to the unusually sturdy constitution of that revered person the death of poor Ivy), but also, in the end – thanks to the First Lady's sudden and very public loss of dignity and the will of her husband to use his influence (which was considerable) in revenge – brought, through a sudden loss of bookings, an end to Bubba's daddy's theatrical career. From that day on, calls to former friends on the fair circuit remained hurtfully unreturned and eyes were averted in his presence. Finally, a broken man, he retired from the business and returned to his father's store, where, one morning in May barely two years later, while fulfilling an order for a quarter-pound of jelly beans, he was heard to emit a strange kind of whistling sound (a sound later – and often – described as 'unearthly' by Jetta Straw who'd ordered the candy), and then seen to disappear behind the counter, where, on a multi-colored carpet of candy, he died. Even today, I can still remember the news when it came and the sadness of that funeral in the rain. The rain marble-bouncing off that box, the chorus of crows in the trees: it all still comes back to me – this and so much else – in great waves of memory under which sometimes I feel I must surely drown.

But I never do. Despite all that has happened (all that I have done) I am sitting here Christmas Eve contemplating these eggs, this bacon, these beans. Despite everything, despite, often, my own best efforts, and though so much around me has died – so many dreams – I still sit here waiting, still moving, still breathing, still alive.

7.40

Man with a Mission

It seems the more I remember of yesterday the harder it is to hold on to the details of the minutes just passed. Oh, sure I can still see Bubba's daddy falling (though in fact I never saw it at all) and sure I can still feel the bumping of Gilber Creek's truck as he drove me away into town – I can see all that like it's happening now – but what about now? For example, that ladder. Remember the ladder, Remember the ladder, I've been telling myself all morning – so what happens? I pull on these overalls and Raymond's old boots (Remember the ladder, I'm still telling myself) and I get all the way out to the barn without it. Just stand here is what I do, trying to figure like an idiot what it is I've forgotten. There's something I know, but I just can't think what. All I can think about is Bubba and those jelly beans and how yesterday he wouldn't stop crying. Jesus Christ. You'd think the way he was wailing that Holly was a person and not just some damn bird. And would he stop, even when I told him that coming with me for a bird that's been shot out of a cannon is no big deal? He would not. (Okay, so it was Ivy that got blasted from the cannon – but what the hell.) He just kept on blubbing and begging and saying he'd do anything in a way that was more pathetic than I can possibly describe. In the end of course he did stop, which was a blessing, but not before he'd had lights coming on across the street and a thumping creeping into my head which took till I was near halfway home to pass away. And even then there was Holly chirping away like she was going on some picnic – so at no point could you say that the evening was in any way peaceful, which by then was just about what I needed.

All of which is of course (as you say) some way from the point – the point being this ladder, the elusiveness of which has caused me this late start.

But – as you say – better late than never.

So.

Starting here – Louie's corner – it's banging these nails in until

139

the job's done – until, finally, Billy Songhurst, once the son of the Minstrel of Moosic, can finally welcome the falling of snow and all that for certain now will be coming in its wake.

10.00

Walk Around the World

It was way back on the day of my leaving that I first heard this story, and so why it returns to me now I have no idea. Perhaps it's a sudden silence that needs filling – this sudden ceasing of my hammer – I don't know. Perhaps it's nothing at all. Anyway, whatever, it comes to me now in this moment of idleness as I sit here at the foot of this ladder, and goes as follows.

Once upon a time there was this man – an inmate of some institution – who passed his time by walking in his mind around the world. Every day he'd walk briskly – always the same route – around the Institute's garden, every day counting his steps. Then, every night, while the rest of the inmates were playing cards or watching TV, he'd pull out an old school atlas and, substituting a mile for every step he'd taken, he'd chart his progress first across America and then over the ocean to the rest of the world. At first his progress seemed real slow – so slow that he even thought of quitting – but then, mile by mile and day by day, he found himself inching on the map heading west until, with nearly a year having passed, he was walking through China and marveling at some old temple, with the miles passing by him like they were nothing. Six months later and India came and went, and with it that country's own sights and smells. Greece then, then Italy moved around him in that garden, until he found himself walking down some wide street in Paris, France. 'Bonjour,' he said to some people passing by, and then the city fell away and he was walking through country and then over a wide body of water, his sights set firmly on Miss Liberty's flame. At first, then, this new city made him fearful, but then something told him in his heart he was safe – nearly home – and he started to walk with his old loose-limbed ease. By now three years had passed in his walking – three years filled with new sights and strange sounds – and a needing rose in him to tell someone what he'd seen, a needing so strong that by the time Virginia was behind him and Kentucky and he was crossing one morning the

Oklahoma state line, he knew he might slip straightway into craziness if he didn't find someone to tell. So he tried. He'd step up to a colleague and start a tale about Russia – how the ice in that country is as blue as summer skies – but that colleague would always move away. At group meetings he'd try to turn the talk around to travel, but his efforts were always ignored. Soon, having met with no success – having found not a soul prepared to even tolerate his talking – he took to grabbing at arms and shouting. 'But I've been to London!' he'd call out at the top of his voice, but no one would listen. Whatever he said, whatever he did, he was met with the same willful incomprehension. Still, though, he persevered until, driven by a frustration almost too acute to bear, he climbed one afternoon to the top of the building and made his way out to the roof, from where, with the aid of a loud-hailer snatched from the band room, he intended to speak of his travels so loudly that all would be forced, whether they liked it or not, to listen and so acknowledge the breadth of his experience of the world. So, balanced then on the ledge, he raised up the hailer and was just drawing breath sufficient to begin when some quality of stillness in the air drew over him, drawing from him all thought of speech and covering him with a slow creeping clearness of eye. 'O Lord,' he whispered and he let go the hailer, heard it smash on the hard ground below. He covered his eyes against the glare of the sun as his eyes strained to take in the vastness of the view. He blinked, felt a stiffness in his limbs and the sickness of self-knowledge in his stomach as he thought of his own self-deceiving. He thought of the years, and the years chilled his blood. 'O sweet Jesus,' he said and he covered his eyes. From that day forward, he never walked again and only once ever uttered a sound. Once, during coverage on TV of some Olympic walking final, he rose unexpectedly to his feet and said 'Spikes,' but nothing more, and three weeks later he was dead.

So? you say, as I did. Jarring along on the day of my leaving on the springs of Gilber Creek's old Bronco pick-up, I studied the old man's face for explanation, but none came. It was, he said, just a story. 'But what does it mean?' I said. 'Mean?' he said, and he laughed. 'Nothin',' he said and he turned on the radio and let the wheel slither like an eel through his hands.

That night, waiting on a ride, I couldn't get the story out of my head. I couldn't stop seeing that old guy standing on that ledge and hearing the crash of that hailer. I couldn't stop thinking of him covering his eyes and I felt in my own limbs the foolishness he'd felt at his dreaming, and when at last there were headlights and the sounds of slowing down and a door swinging out I bundled into that car so fast that even now, sitting here at the foot of this ladder in silence, I swear I can still feel the rushing of that night air, still hear the sweet cocoon-slamming of that door.

But listen to me going on – just sitting here on a break talking when there's still so much to do. You know someone looking on might think Billy Songhurst was a slacker in his work, or reluctant even to get that work done. Which of course could not be further from reality.

Rest for the Weary

So there it is, the last bolt in, the end of this particular road. I suppose some kind of celebration would be the thing now, although, what with this no-drinking policy, just about all that's left to do as far as celebrating is concerned is not much. I suppose I could go back to the house and fix something different to eat (maybe a piece of that steak Bubba said he was keeping for special), although as far as that goes I'm not sure right now I've got the energy, all this climbing and hammering having taken the toll that it has. In fact right now all I really feel like doing is just sitting down and watching TV (there's Oprah every day at noon, at least on regular days), maybe listen to some music on the radio. Oh, sure, I know it's Christmas Eve and all that and there're things I could be doing, but to tell you the truth right now I just don't seem to be able to care, which is strange. After all, getting this job done I always thought would be some kind of high point – there'd be some kind of feeling of real satisfaction – when in fact, now it's done, I can tell you I've scarcely felt lower. Which is not to say of course that the feeling's going to last, although so far it's been doing a good job. For maybe two hours now it's been coming on – ever since that break and my thinking about Gilber Creek and that story of his, which I knew at the time was a mistake, but I just couldn't stop myself. Anyway, there was that, and then I got to thinking how I never did get the phone connected at the store and what if maybe someone's been trying to reach me while I've been out here hammering and all they've been getting is some kind of tone that says nobody's home. Without wanting to I kept thinking maybe there's been trouble at the Pen or maybe some kind of accident on the road. And then there was Holly and wondering again just exactly what Bubba meant when he said, You'll see, and if maybe – given the circumstances – giving her to Audacity as a present is maybe not so wise. After all, if a bird who can already whistle 'Hail to the Chief' while dancing on a hotplate is said to have some special talent, then that special talent could be just about anything. For all I know she can maybe do impressions or fly backwards or something, or maybe when Audacity opens the wrapping she'll find Holly sitting back with the *Washington Post* and smoking a bird-sized cigar. Anyway, whatever, standing high on that ladder, I got to convincing myself that the whole idea's a bust and that as far as a gift is concerned I better think of something else and quick. But of course I couldn't think of anything, and I still can't. Which is making me think right now that maybe I've got no choice and I'll just have to take a chance and hope that Holly isn't some kind of suicide bird with a special thing for redheads, and that she'll just do as she's told and sing sweet like I've been trying to teach her. All of which then, combined with the fact that today is Alice's birthday – or would be – accounts for this feeling of heaviness I mentioned. You know sitting here now, listening to the wind on the roof, it's like my arms and legs are filled up with sand and I couldn't move them even if I wanted to. You know right now I don't think I could move even if Audacity were to walk in that door and say 'Hi.' In fact, I feel suddenly so tired now that you'll have to forgive me if I just close my eyes for a second. Yes I know it's only noon, but I feel like I've been up for days. Right now I feel like I've been moving heavy through some dream, like I've been walking and walking through years without end.

In the Beginning

Sometimes I try to think of how things might have been, try to imagine myself in some other parallel life – and I can for a while, though it never lasts. For a while sometimes I can see myself with a job and a wife and a family and a car in a garage and a neat front lawn. And sometimes I see myself coming home on a Friday night, sitting patient at the lights with gifts for the children on the seat beside me and the sound of a band in the distance. I pull over on a wide street in the shade of broad trees and watch as the band passes by, cymbals crashing and drums thumping low. I feel myself smiling, then the smooth of the road beneath my wheels. And then, always, just as I'm turning, just as I'm feeling the bumping of my driveway, I feel something shifting inside me then the color drains away and then everything's gone. Always I'm back then, left with nothing but the way things are, with what I've become, my path, with Alice and the day of her passing.

Now, today, silence is what I recall of that day, and the silence of the days following. The days seemed to creep by with barely a word being spoken. Only Aunt Celeste, it seemed, had the breath to speak and the strength (given to her, she said, by God) to break that silence. Every morning I'd wake to the clashing of pots and pans and the sound of her singing from below. 'He touched me,' she'd sing, her voice rising high above the clashing, 'He touched me and made me whole.' Standing at my window, with Larry still snoring in his bed (not even Aunt Celeste could rouse him from his sleeping), I'd look out across the yard, searching for my daddy, half expecting to see him bending over Uncle Braxton's old John Deere or maybe banging in fenceposts at the top of Salter's Field. I'd squint at the far trees, half imagining I could see him moving through the shadows, or tell myself he'd just taken the pick-up into town and that any minute now he'd be coming back down that road, moving slow on the hard ground, the truck full of rolls of barbwire or feed for the chickens. Then, when he didn't appear, when there was only Uncle Braxton in the fields, I'd lie back on my bed and just listen to Larry's snoring. I'd try to think of where Daddy might be – where he went so early every morning and came back from so late every night – but nothing – only a blankness – would come. In a while then, every morning, Aunt Celeste would quit her banging and there'd be footsteps in the hall and the slow drift of bacon, then her voice calling breakfast up the stairs.

Breakfast on those days – the days that followed Alice's death – was just me and Uncle Braxton, Aunt Celeste and Larry. Mama's place would be laid and Daddy's too, but they never appeared and nobody asked why. It was like suddenly they were invisible – like they were sitting there alright but just nobody could see them – and like being invisible was just about the most normal thing in the world. Even Uncle Braxton said nothing in those first weeks – even when he suddenly had no one to help him and the extra work kept him out till after dusk – he'd just sit there at the table with that newspaper of his propped up against the salt, the corner of his eye twitching every time Aunt Celeste tried to interest him in talk. He'd just sit there, eyes flicking left and then right across the print, until Aunt Celeste'd give up with a smile and a nod like she'd received a perfectly good answer to some question and at last at least *that* was settled, and then she'd start clearing the dishes and soon she'd start her singing at the sink. 'What a friend we have in Jesus,' she'd sing out over the suds, singing on when the back door slammed and Uncle Braxton crossed the yard and only pausing at the tooting of the school bus on the highway as she shooed me and Larry from the house. All the way to school, I recall, I used to wonder what Aunt Celeste used to do in the house all day, now that Mama never left her room – whether she ever stopped her singing for one thing or whether that singing was just for our benefit – something for us all to wake up to and to drift off to last thing at night – and if when we were gone she just fell into silence. I used to picture her there, just standing staring out across the sink, sometimes climbing the stairs to Mama's room. Here, in my mind's eye, she'd sit light on the bedclothes and she and Mama would share secrets. They'd talk, of course, about Daddy – about where he went every day and what he might be doing when he should have been helping Uncle Braxton – and the more I heard them in

the ear of my mind, the more their voices came to me on that bus
– the more certain I became that they were hiding something from
me – that they knew all along where he went every day and that
they were just trying to fool me with their talking. In short, their
secrets, I became certain, were secrets kept from me, and I deter-
mined to find out what they were.

It was in early February, with the ground still hard mid-morning
with the frost, that one day I doubled back from the school gates
and walked the four or so miles back from town. I turned off the
track and made my way around the edge of West Field. From here,
like some Indian scout, I circled the old well and crept into the
shadow at the side of the house. Edging to the corner, I peered
around. There, standing ticking in the yard, was Daddy's old pick-
up, its tires still wet from the frost. I stared at the mist rising off of
its hood, tried to figure the sense of what I saw. But sense wouldn't
come – just a slow creeping coolness on my skin. That Daddy was
a part of things too – that he too was deceiving me – was crazy I
knew and I scowled at the thought, tried to shift it. But it wouldn't
get shifted. It just sat there in my mind leering at me, laughing at
me for having been so dumb. *See*, it seemed to say to me, and I felt
my heart slow. Overhead, the winter sky seemed to darken.

With the coolness of a thief, I eased open the screen door, eased
it back against the frame behind me. The hall was in shadow, Aunt
Celeste's coat and boots gone from the rack. I froze at the sound of
muffled voices from above, the sound of footsteps on boards. I
waited, held my breath, the footsteps ceased. Slowly then, mindful
of the creaks on the stairs, I made my way up to the landing, eased
myself along the wall to Mama's door. The voices now – Mama's
and Daddy's – were louder now but muffled. I put my ear to the
door. At first there was nothing – just silence – then I heard Daddy
say how something meant nothing. His voice seemed close at hand
– maybe just the other side of the door – but then it drifted, grew
faint. Listening hard, I heard him say Was it true? Was it really not
him? Then Mama said something I didn't hear. For a while then
there was nothing, then the sound again of boots getting closer. I
stepped back, turned the handle of Aunt Celeste's room behind me,
closed the door just in time. Boots then, growing fainter on the
stairs, the screen door banging. I edged open the door. Across

the hall, Mama's door was open. She was lying on her bed, her arms across her eyes, her skin so pale and her shoulders heaving with crying or cold. I crossed the hall, stood still in the doorway, my ear tuned fine to a pick-up's growling engine. 'Mama?' I said. She lowered her arms, heaved up her head. 'Billy?' she said. Her pale face was streaked with tears. She held out her arms, but something froze me. 'Where's Daddy going?' I said, and in that moment I knew that he too had been deceived – that something had been kept from him also. 'Billy?' said Mama again, but I was already turning, already on the stairs, already running hard down the hall and out into the freezing air, already pounding hard, my feet slapping on the track, already calling out, my voice whipping back behind me and my eyes streaming, stinging with tears.

The truck when I reached it was pulled over to one side, Daddy looking hard straight ahead.

'Go back,' he said.

'Where're you going?' I said, I could hardly speak for gasping. I reached a hand through the window and tried to hold him back by the shoulder, but he pulled away.

'Listen,' he said, he flicked his eyes to mine. They flicked away, something unsaid. Instead he told me to take care of my mama, and then the engine was raving and the wheels spinning hard and then I was standing on that track looking up towards the trees, watching that truck growing smaller and smaller until it was gone and there was nothing – nothing to say it had ever been here, no sign that it had ever existed – no sign that my daddy had ever existed – save for the smell of gasoline hanging still in the moist air and the fast-melting tracks on the road.

4.15

The Long Season

So early these days the days close in. By four already the light's losing its grip, giving way to the dusk that comes rolling through the trees, tumbling over roots and breaching ruined fence lines. No longer – not for years it seems now – summer's benediction; all now is darkness, its grip squeezing tight like gloved hands, choking, smothering all hope in this the long season.

Waiting.

This, now, the character of days.

Waiting for Daddy at that upstairs window, for Audacity here in this barn. Here, in Louie's corner, I stand, barely daring to breathe, my ears tuned for sounds on that highway. None, so far, comes. All that comes is the rattling of this wind – how it snarls, defeated, around my new-bolted sanctuary. Hear how it circles, creeping suddenly like a thief, feel its cool leering breath on my cheek. *Step out*, it whispers, *There's someone here to see you.* No, I say, but I look anyway, and of course there is no one.

Waiting, always waiting.

And sometimes these days, the days seem to move so slow that I can feel my blood slowing, feel it cooling until it sits cold as ice in my veins. And sometimes – with hours dragging by – I step out and watch myself moving – hours for minutes – slow like a man moving heavy underwater. For endless hours I watch myself – sometimes standing again on that Arkansas hillside, or laughing hollow again at the store. But most times I just stand here waiting – longing for what's coming – what I'm due – while at the same time scarcely able to believe what I've done, scarcely able to believe that this man in the mirror is me.

5.00

Barricaded

Well five o'clock already and, as you can see, I'm still here. Which is not to say I've been idle. No, sir. I have, as you can see, been at work. Doing what? Well I suggest you try those doors. Those doors – if you can get to them through all that stuff – have never I believe been so secure. In fact, right now, I believe that not even Raymond could get through. Right now I believe that there's not a man born who could get to me now.

5.48

Don't Think I Don't Know

Okay okay, don't think I don't know that if I open up these doors and step out of this barn then bang goes any credibility I may have left. Don't think I don't know this. Also, don't think I don't know what you're thinking. You're thinking, So fine, he locks himself up real tight in that barn aiming to wait for something – somebody – that may or may not come, and then, thanks to his not thinking about food or how exactly he's planning to survive in this cold (I have with me, as you've so cleverly noticed, no blankets and not even Raymond's old jacket), combined with an unconnected telephone ringing so loud it can be heard through this terrible wind, he's standing here now peering out through these slats like he's some kind of convict on the run and any minute there'll be loud-hailers and agents from the ATF or FBI or some such organization getting ready to bust their way in like they don't seem to be able to stop themselves doing these days. Well, that's your business and, frankly, you can think what you like. Consistency, after all, in my view is overrated. I mean, you only have to look at Larry for proof of that. For sure no one's more consistent than him – especially when it comes to getting into trouble. Take, for example, his current situation. I mean even for him (and whichever way you look at it), being forty-one years old but still being fool enough to get yourself caught breaking into that State Pentitentiary five miles from Elk City with enough tools of the safe-breaking trade that you'd think it was Fort Knox he was aiming for and not some goddamn cashbox that it turns out had nothing in it anyhow on account of the prisoners having been paid that morning for their license plates or whatever the hell it is they get paid for, is some kind of triumph in the Being Consistently a Fool stakes – especially when it turns out the day he settles upon to commit his ingenious crime is a fine summer's day in early July and that day to be precise is the fourth.

Independence Day.

Exactly.

Some independence.

So don't talk to me about being consistent. Being consistent can get you into all kinds of *strife*.

But like I say, anyway if I go or stay it really is none of your business. Besides, I haven't gone yet. Despite the ringing of that phone (Jesus, I never could bear to let a phone ring), I'm still standing here, still buttoned up tight in this barn. And – believe me – I know what you're thinking about that: don't think that I don't. Don't think I don't know that you're thinking I'm scared – that you're thinking I'm standing here shoulder to the slats just listening out for Bubba in the yard. No, sir. Don't think I don't know that you're thinking I'm thinking it's Raymond – and that I don't know that you're thinking that I'm thinking that any second he'll be by, now it's dark, to get his revenge. No, sir – don't you think I don't know, 'cause I know alright. Don't you go thinking I'm as dumb as Larry. Nobody's as dumb as that brother of mine. I mean, Jesus Christ, ain't nobody breaks *in*. People break *out* real regular – do it all the time. But break in? Shoot. Ain't nobody breaks in. Nobody except Larry. You know sometimes it seems like having a brother is just about the worst thing that can happen to a man. Aside, of course, from having a daddy who never knew you were alive, and now never will.

But that's another story. For now, I shall try not to dwell on that or anything else that's not casting some positive light. Gloom and doom right now is not what I need. What I need right now – what I could really use – is just an hour maybe of sunshine, or maybe just a few minutes of the moon.

6.00

Old Scores

Six bells and still nothing but that ringing. Whoever it is they sure are persistent. I mean you'd think by now they'd have got the message – figured Christmas Eve and rung off. But no. Still it goes on – do you hear it? – ring, ring ring . . .

Just ignore it, you say. Well maybe you're right – maybe I should – but that's easier said than done. I mean what if something's happened? What if there's been some kind of an accident and Audacity's lying somewhere in some emergency room and they're trying to reach me?

Okay, okay. You're right. There's no place here for panicking. You're right – staying calm is the thing. And anyway – as you say – nobody knows I'm here, do they? – so why would they be calling me? No, sir. Best to stay put – keep an eye out. It's Christmas Eve after all – the season of goodwill. What better time for a person to sneak up on a person? What better time than now for a person to settle old scores?

6.42

Listen

There – that sound again. Did you hear it? No? Well listen . . .
   There.
   And there.
   The sound of a motor – far off but getting closer – drifting in and out on the wind.
   Jesus Christ.
   What do you mean, take a look? What do you think I've been doing? You think I've been standing here daydreaming?

8.25

Christmas Truce

Well I really must say how terrific the place looks. Though I say it myself, there is about it now a spirit of fun and even homeliness that even I, before I began this evening, would have said would be just about impossible, given the circumstances, to achieve. It just goes to show I suppose what a few decorations can do – not to mention no small amount of will – all of which I'll admit has taken its toll. Not that I'm begrudging the effort, you understand – quite the contrary. While it's true that my arms now are real achy thanks to their having to assume and hold for some time the unusual positions necessary to get the paper-chains fixed in those loops to the ceilings, and I could have done without losing my footing and tumbling that time like a fool off Jacob's ladder with the consequence that I've bruised up my left knee real bad, I will be the first to say (and here I go again singing my own praises – but what the hell) that nearly a small miracle has been achieved here – and in such a short time too. In fact, to be absolutely truthful, I cannot recall one time in the past when this parlor (not to mention the rest of the house, which I'll show you in due course – and believe me it's worth seeing) ever looked as festive if you like and welcoming as it surely does this evening. Not once, for example (at least in my memory) were we ever allowed such a grand-looking tree or so many candles – or even a real fire like that in the grate. You know sometimes, looking back, I find it hard to recall what exactly we *did* do in this house to celebrate the season – which meant of course what Uncle Braxton would let us do, the house being his to decorate (or not decorate) and you better not forget it. Oh for sure I have a memory way back of some kind of tree and maybe a few lights (the result of weeks and weeks of Aunt Celeste's persuading), but there was nothing ever as grand as today's display.

But hey. It's the Christmas season and the Christmas season is a time of forgiving if it's anything. So: if you're listening, Uncle Braxton, wherever you are, I forgive you, okay? Please hear now that I forgive you for all that you did and didn't do – for being such a mean-spirited old man and for just about ruining the family which God in His wisdom gave you. Not, of course, that God had anything to do with it as far as you were concerned – oh no. To you (and how many times did you try to tell us this?) there was no God – no plan – and therefore no need for this season of forgiving. It was all, you said, just fantasy and lies – just something to keep folks from seeing the truth – which was what? Which was, you said, that there's no guiding hand – however much we want there to be one – and that everybody, in the end, is alone. And for proof of this? That island, the war, those soldiers with their sallow skins, the pain. How can there be a God, you'd say – an all-powerful, all-loving Father – when there's so much deceit and pain in this world? When a man can be standing beside you one minute and the next you're wearing his guts like an overcoat? How? you'd say, and you'd stare at us, those eyes of yours burning, until Larry'd start crying and I'd feel like crying too . . .

But – as I say – I forgive you. For all this, and for resenting my daddy so (was it just his traveling you envied and hated so – the chaos and carelessness of his life – or was there more?) – but most of all for telling him the truth – for turning my daddy in a minute into a stranger and setting him on the road to that river and the end; for all this and more, I forgive you. It is, after all, Christmas. And, after all, it's not as if I don't have other things right now to concern me. Right now, aside from looking after Holly (not to mention the Big Guy), there is the little matter of tomorrow's menu. As I'm sure you're aware, food – especially a turkey with all the trimmings – does not prepare itself. In fact, right now – or rather once, at last, I've fixed up these lights – I think perhaps it might be wise if I devoted a little time now ahead of time to the matter of that bird and its needs. I seem to remember something about an hour a pound and then one more for luck or the pot or something. Anyway, I guess I can always ask.

So. Forgive me now will you if I just shut down for a while and get these lights fixed. You cannot, after all, have a tree without lights – nor (and here I'm sure you'll agree) would Christmas be Christmas without a little Christmas spirit. So cheers. Here's to it.

Here's to tonight and that snow I've been promised, and all that its coming must surely bring.

You Never Can Tell

Well that Holly sure is one perverse bird. There she was singing for hours with nobody to listen, but now – as soon as there's an audience – nothing. Hotplate on, hotplate off: nothing makes no difference. She just sits there with her head pulled in close and kind of guilty-looking – which you could understand in a person what with the trouble that's been caused – but in a bird? I don't mind telling you it's news to me that canaries (even though they are, according to Bubba, the brightest of birds) have any thoughts in their heads besides eating and shitting thoughts – but then I suppose that just goes to show that it's not just people that can surprise you, but birds also and God knows what else. I guess there really is truth in the phrase 'You never can tell.' With birds like Holly for sure. It's just as well for her that there's no law in this state against impersonating a telephone, otherwise she'd be for sure so locked up now that even that Birdman of Alcatraz would seem like some short-term inmate. All of which, of course, is somewhat off the point, the point being I was hoping for some company right now, what with the time dragging by like this and nothing to do but wait. Oh, sure, there's plenty of stuff I could be doing (should be doing) – a whole heap of dusting for one thing, not to mention a shine that needs fixing to these shoes – and I suppose I should be upstairs again by now to check up on the patient; I can't, though, seem to work up the will. Partly, I'm sure, it's it being Christmas Eve and this feeling of being on the verge of things that that brings. Partly, also, it's the feeling of this house – a sense of eyes upon you wherever you go – that no amount of baubles or paper-chains or Christmas lights can shift. But mostly, mostly, I'll admit it's all this thinking about Audacity that seems, at the moment at least, to have sapped my energy and brought on me this need suddenly for company. However hard I try I can't stop myself thinking how she's out in that world somewhere – living and breathing – maybe headed this way, and how maybe soon – in just a matter of hours maybe – she'll be standing in this hallway and breathing this air that I'm breathing. I'd stop thinking like this if I could, believe me – it just drags things out, makes the time go so slow – but with this silence all around I can't seem to make it. Creep, creep, creep, the hands of this spiteful old clock – and no word still from Holly. Still she sits there, staring at me as I'm staring at her, her neck all bunched up like she's reading my thoughts and is not impressed. Cocky bird. You know sometimes I don't think she quite realizes the dynamics of the particular situation she's in. I don't think she's aware sometimes of just how easy it would be for me to lose my temper and do something I might regret. But then again, maybe she knows about this season of goodwill – maybe she senses something benevolent in the air, or maybe (you never can tell) her silence means she can feel something coming that I can't that makes her real sure of herself – but if so, what? Whatever it is, she sure as hell isn't saying, and she's giving no clues in her look. All she does is just sit there staring. Well of that I have just about had enough. For company I might just as well turn on the TV, or even make my way back up those stairs. I mean even the guy upstairs makes some contribution, some effort to bring life to this silence. But not Holly – oh no. What does she do? Nothing. Won't even dance no more. I turn up the plate, but nothing. She just sits there staring back, unblinking, like she's daring me to be first to look away, like it's all just some kind of game. Jesus Christ. Talk about a waste of space. You know I reckon there's just about nothing that's worse than a bird that won't sing.

Sneaky Moon

So quiet at night when the furnace shuts down. Like now, standing here at this window, there's nothing but my breathing and the breathing way off of the blue-black fields. For a second the moon spills its light across the yard, then – frightened it seems – slips back behind the barn and all again is dark. Somewhere a fox barks dryly in some trees; I turn at a whisper behind me, cross the room, ease my ear close, listen hard. Nothing, again – just imagination, just a whisper, just Bubba lying still.

Oh, I know what you're thinking. You're thinking how come Bubba's lying there behind me on Aunt Celeste's bed, and how come he's got that bump on his head that's ballooning like it is. Well don't look at me. If he hadn't have pulled up in that pick-up when he did and if it hadn't have been so dark (not to mention the fact of the state of some anxiety things quite beyond my control had gotten me into), then what happened would likely never have happened. I mean, Jesus. How could I possibly have known it was him creeping across that yard and not some person with some real bad intention? And anyway, it's not as if I didn't shout out that warning like I did, or use as they say strictly minimal force with that broom handle, is it now? No, sir, it is not. The fact is I didn't and there's really nothing I can do about it right now – and besides, if Bubba really was doing a bad thing and trying to deceive me by sneaking up on me then I guess he got pretty much what was coming to him anyway and he really can't complain. But – like I say – crazy thoughts. I mean, am I to blame if he can't take a joke? I am not. Neither am I to blame for that voice in my head that went and told him such outrageous lies and called it confessing. No, sir. That so-called confessing was just the whispering of the season, just the lies of this cool sneaky deceiving moon.

Sunday

5.30

Light of the World

Wake to a vision of Jesus. He stands – light of the world – at the foot of my bed, arms outstretched in empty embrace, his robes as white as the land. I close my eyes hard, open them; he is gone. I turn. The door, a tilted chair, stand as they were, a barricade. I turn back, hear the rustle, loud, of my head on the pillow. 'Today's the day,' says a voice – none other but my own. It vibrates in my ear, hangs muffled in the cold air, is gone.

7.30

Idle Hands

You'll understand when I tell you that the Doctor was absolutely the last person I expected to see just now on my return from Salter's Field. But – sure enough – there he was, pale-faced on that screen, wrists and ankles in chains and his eyes kind of starey like he could hardly believe it himself. He was moving like a ghost – half dragging – just a bag of bones between two officers, each of whom was so big it was like that's why they were chosen, so they'd make him look small. Even now I can scarcely believe it. And to think I'd just been thinking of him too – the way he was the last time I saw him – trying to picture the details of that room of his and the way he had of smiling that made you think he knew something you didn't (which he probably did) – trying to think of anything and everything in fact so as to keep my mind off of the present so the time wouldn't drag so and whatever time is remaining before Audacity comes is just going to be gone and she'll be here. And it was working too – just as the Doctor used to say it would. 'Time won't fly if you watch it,' he used to say, and, 'Idle hands are hands that need winding.' I'd even got to forgetting the hardness of that ground and the weight even before it was lifting anything of Uncle Braxton's old shovel; in fact, I'd been thinking so hard about those bird pictures on the walls and that desk of his with the top so out of whack you could lay down a pencil one end and catch it two seconds later dropping off of the other that I got that hole dug and filled even before I knew it and soon I was staring down into that darkness and thinking maybe I should say a prayer. In the end though I said nothing – I just stood there with my head bowed and my hands kind of clasped – all the time trying to keep my mind filled with stuff – and not just the Doctor. No, sir. As I beat down the earth with the flat of that spade and jabbed in that cross I let my mind scoot to wherever it pleased – to anywhere in fact that would keep the minutes marching and the future, every minute, coming closer. One minute there was Larry, sitting Christmas morning alone in his cell (in my mind's eye he was opening his gift – tears in his eyes and tearing at the paper like a kid); then the next there was Raymond, standing hunched over in the gloom of that latrine, this thick winter coat wrapped around him like a shroud and his voice – *I ain't goin', But you gotta, Well I ain't* – creeping muffled through the damp wooden slats. Standing there this morning just looking down at that fresh earth, it was like the past was all fresh too and I was seeing it again for the first time. For the first time again I was watching Uncle Braxton put his hand on Raymond's shoulder, and again I heard him say he was sorry. *Too many hands*, he was saying, *Too many mouths now*, and then he was scowling, looking down, and Raymond was shaking his head and saying he had no place to go. Then Raymond was turning again as he'd turned on that day, then walking away through the barn's open door and out across this yard.

You know, thinking about it now, standing here where he stood for a long moment that day looking around real close like he knew he was seeing things for the last time and he wanted to remember, it's funny but I can't stop that same feeling too: I can't shift the feeling that I'm living right now – right this minute, these seconds – through an hour of change and that soon all I've known will be gone forever – the past buried as it should be by an onrushing future.

8.53

Demolition Man

Well I'd never have guessed how hard it is to break up a bed. A chest of drawers is one thing – but a bed: Jesus! You know I reckon what with all the bolts and stuff and the wood joints and the way they've gotten so tight – so jammed – with all those years of Mama's weight on them, not even a professional demolition man could have gotten the thing apart and into furnace-size pieces like this without cutting up his hands real bad like mine – not to mention collecting all these splinters that no way am I ever gonna get out if it's not in some emergency room with some doctor with like amazing eyesight. I mean some of these things are so goddamn small that I can't even see them – just feel them – all of which I know sounds crazy when you consider the size of that bed. And, believe me, I wouldn't have tackled it at all if there'd been anything else left up there made of wood (except the fire surround, that is: even I'm not so crazy – so desperate to lose these hands altogether – that I'll ever tackle that), but I've used just about everything – and, besides, I had to do something what with this furnace just about out and hollering like some kind of crazy child that's starving. You know, standing here now just looking at it and seeing how calm it is now it's been fed, it's tough to believe just how crazy it can get and how much it can eat when it gets started. I mean, take now. You see this mean little pile? Well, bolts aside, that's just about all that's left now of Mama's bed. You know, standing here, listening to that grinding and feeling that heat that's just starting to rise through the house, it occurs to me that if I don't get my act together and find some other outside source of fuel (maybe those trees at the top of the track – but I'd need an ax for that, not to mention the will and new hands), then sooner or later I'll have burnt just about everything I can in this house, and all Mr Crazy here'll be left with will be this nice wooden house itself . . .

Oh I know what you're thinking. You're thinking not even Barking Billy's that crazy. You're thinking even he'd stop short of

171

burning down a house just to feed an old furnace so that house can get heated. Well. News for you is what I got. After all, I'm so crazy, remember, that I went on believing that my daddy was my daddy even when I knew in my heart that he wasn't, so crazy that I didn't see what I saw when I saw Uncle Braxton and the way he looked at Mama with the longing of some lost child – and so crazy that I stood in that Amarillo parking lot watching Audacity and our child inside her driving away, and so crazy that I chased her and held her on that hillside so tight she was begging me to stop. But I couldn't stop – can't still, even in my dreams.

Oh, I know what you're thinking. I'm thinking it too. I'm thinking burning a house down would be the least of my crimes. In fact I'm thinking maybe it's the least I could do, that maybe after all I should take a match to this bottle of kerosene, maybe once and for all make a difference in this world – light a fire so bright and so hot that it shadows and scorches this land and leaves nothing behind it but ashes and dust.

Oh and yes I know what you're thinking.

You're thinking, Go on.

You're thinking, One strike and it's done.

You're thinking, Do it.

You're thinking, Now.

2.23

Merry Christmas Mr Songhurst

This morning, during Personal Time, I was flipping the channels on the Rec Room TV, just searching for Oprah, when I came across this preacher who was talking about Heaven. Heaven, he was saying, and he was raising a finger and stabbing upwards, wasn't there, but here (here he started jabbing at his chest) – here, right here in the heart of man. It was, he said, a place to which all are invited but for which only a few are provided with maps. Which of course, he said, was where he came in. For a fee of only nineteen ninety-nine (all credit cards accepted, calls toll-free), he, the Reverend Sheets of Plainview, Arkansas, Chief Minister of the Church of the Holy Surprise, would reveal to each and every one of us the secrets of that map. 'Call now,' he said, he was holding his hands out, palms upward, imploring, 'and come join His People in Heaven!'

And people called. As I sat there with my morning drink growing cold in my hand, I watched as the Reverend Sheets stepped back with a sureness and stood beside a table that had on it a bright red phone. 'O Lord,' he started whispering. 'O Lord, O Lord, O Lord – ' Then a smile spread over his face as the phone started ringing. He lifted the receiver.

'Hello?' he said.

For a moment there was silence on the line – maybe just the faint sound of breathing – then a woman's voice, tiny, said, 'Reverend?'

The Reverend closed his eyes, he seemed to be whispering something.

'Reverend?' said the woman again, 'is you there?' Her voice was even smaller now – like whatever courage she'd had was draining fast.

'Oh, child,' said the Reverend at last, he was frowning hard like he was concentrating real hard, 'are you lost, child? Are you needing the Lord's direction?'

174

For a moment again there was silence – just a crackling on the line. Then the woman said, 'Is it far?'

'Far, child?' said the Reverend.

'To well, you know – ' said the woman, hesitating.

'Child?' said the Reverend. Then he placed the palm of his free hand on his temple, like he was trying to sense something over the miles. 'Is it Heaven you're meaning, child?' he said.

Well the woman started stammering then, but the Reverend cut her off. 'Well the answer is yes!' he said, 'Yes! Yes! Yes!'

'Yes?' said the woman.

Then the Reverend sighed. 'And no,' he said.

'No?' said the woman.

'Yes,' said the Reverend, 'it is far – but only as far as the borders of love!'

Another silence, then the Reverend said, 'Child?'

'You mean – ' said the woman, hesitating again.

'Oh!' cried the Reverend. 'Speak up, child – speak up!'

'You mean,' she said, 'it's further than Rush Springs?'

Well the Reverend looked stumped. 'What?' he said, and for a moment his composure dipped. 'Look,' he started, a trace of anger now in his voice, but then he straightened himself up and started smiling again. 'Oh, child,' he said, 'child,' and he lowered his hand then, placed it over his heart. 'Are you ready, child,' he said, 'for the journey?'

'Well – ' said the woman. You could tell she wasn't sure.

Then the Reverend frowned suddenly. 'Or will you,' he said, 'will you stay lost in the wilderness like Paul?'

'Paul?' said the woman. 'Is he lost?'

'Excuse me?' said the Reverend.

'That Pauly,' she said, 'where'd he go now?'

'What?' said the Reverend. There was a sharpness suddenly in his voice that you could hear down the line when he told her that madam must decide.

There was another pause then as the woman tried to think. Then at last she said, 'Well, okay – ' and the Reverend punched the air. 'Praise the Lord!' he cried, 'Oh, praise the Lord!'

'Reverend?' said the woman.

'Oh, praise, praise the Lord!'

'I'm a senior citizen – '

For the second time then the Reverend cut her off. 'Now,' he said, 'let me pass you on – '

'And I was hoping – '

He hitched up a smile, fixed and hard like an ice-skater's smile. 'Now, child,' he said, 'just stay on the line – '

' . . . special rate . . .'

Slowly, gravely, he set down the phone. It rang again at once. He let it ring twice, three times, four, then picked it up.

'Hello?' he said.

This second caller was a man. His voice was clear – no fuzz, no static – making him sound like he was in the next room.

'Child?' said the Reverend. He smiled. He waited. 'Child,' he said at last, 'are you there?' Again his hand drifted to his temple. Still nothing. Then a clatter on the line – perhaps the caller changing the receiver hand to hand. 'Look,' said the voice at last, 'you say you're a reverend – right?'

'Ordained by the love of Christ,' said the Reverend.

More clattering then the faint sound of coughing. 'Well, Reverend – ' said the man, there was a real leering now in his voice, 'can I ask you a question?'

'Ask away!' said the Reverend. He was smiling still, but a smile suddenly so brittle-looking that you'd think any minute it was bound to shatter, leaving nothing behind it but a faceless head.

'Well how come – ' The man started coughing again, then breathing shallow, rasping. 'How come if God's so smart he lets so many bad things happen to people who ain't done no harm to nobody – how come that happens, huh?'

Well the Reverend Sheets dropped his smile then, replaced it in a moment with a real heavy frown. 'Well, child,' he began, but the coughing on the line forced him to stop; he twitched. Then he squinted at the camera like he was searching out the caller. 'Child,' he said, 'are you sick?'

'Huh?' said the man.

'I said are you sick, child?'

The coughing came again, eased. 'Hello?' said the man. His voice was suddenly faint, far off and moving further like a voice withdrawing in a dream.

'I'm here, child,' said the Reverend.

'Well?' said the man.

The Reverend raised an eyebrow. 'What is it, child?' he said.

Another cough. 'You didn't answer what I asked you. And don't give me none of that mysterious ways crap – '

The Reverend smiled. 'But the ways of the Lord *are* mysterious, child,' he said. 'Mysterious and wonderful – believe me! I know!'

'But – ' said the man, then he said nothing more for the Reverend replaced the receiver.

It was then – this morning – that something strange happened. It was then that the Reverend Wilson Sheets, Chief Minister of the Church of the Holy Surprise, leaned forward and rapped his knuckles on the glass of the Rec Room TV. 'Hey, you,' he said.

'Me?' I said. I looked around: there was nobody else – just Mr McMurtry pushing heavy on a broom down the hall.

'Yes, you,' said the Reverend. He was frowning, almost scowling, his blue-black hair shining in the TV lights though his face was in shadow.

Well I stared. I have spoken to Oprah more times than I can remember, and often to sportscasters during breaks for commercials – but never to a reverend. Jesus, I thought, and I sat myself up. 'What is it?' I said. 'What do you want?'

'Want, son?' said the Reverend. He cast his eyes down, held a beat, looked up. His eyes now were shiny with tears. 'I want you to just take a look at the sky – take a look at the sky, Billy-Boy!'

That, then, an hour ago now, and I have to report that though I've studied these skies until my eyes are real achy I see no more evidence of snow on the way than I've seen these last seven Christmas Eves that have passed since the fire. But then – as the Doctor used to say – you never can tell, so I guess I'll keep looking, keep waiting, and when people come by and ask me as they always do what I'm waiting for I shall tell them what I always tell them. I shall tell them that I'm waiting for a promise to be kept, then I'll watch them smile and I'll watch them move away.